Stolen Sisters

Joyce Phillips

Stolen Sisters

By Joyce Phillips

Copyright 2023 by Joyce Phillips

Layout and Design: RMK Publishing

Phillips, Joyce

Stolen Sisters / by Joyce Phillips

Summary: A grandmother searches the southwest for her kidnapped granddaughter. University students and a Navajo shaman join in the search.

ISBN 978-1-0881-1578-7

Published in the United States of America

In Loving Memory of

Scott Edward Raymond

My son was born on October 30, 1964, and died February 14, 2020. I believe he was at my side while I wrote this book. I grieve for him every day.

PROLOGUE

"My wife did NOT leave me! She's missing." John Tessay jumped from his chair to pound on the scarred wooden desk in front of him. A white coffee mug bounced. Black sludge spilled over the side, while a blue pen rolled off the desk and clattered to the floor. He swayed for a moment on unsteady legs, then reached into his pants pocket for a red bandanna handkerchief and swabbed at the coffee puddle. "Sorry."

"You gotta relax, Mr. Tessay. We need to get information from you." Officer Goseyun rose from behind his desk and faced the man. A silver badge pinned to his chest read: Fort Apache Police Department. A blond wooden plaque on his desk identified him as *Officer Dwayne Goseyun*, the words etched in gold letters.

"John, my name's John." He lowered red-rimmed eyes, tugged at a blue cotton jacket that sat lopsided on his shoulders and returned to his seat. A big man, the energy emanating from his body, appeared to send sparks of fear into the room. "I gave my information last night. Rose went shopping yesterday. She didn't come home. When I call her cell phone, it goes to 'leave a message.'" John scraped a hand across his face. "I called her friends in case she stopped by. No one's seen or heard from her."

Officer Goseyun sat and slid the Attempt to Locate Form across the desk so he could read it. "Last night's report states that you and your wife didn't argue. Why did you think she'd be at a friend's house?"

"Rose belongs to a book club. They meet at different homes. I dunno. I thought maybe she'd run an errand for someone, forgot the time." John rubbed the back of his head. "I tried everything to find her. Our little girl is only three. She needs her mother. Please, find her." His hand shook as he stuffed the wet handkerchief back in his pocket.

The police officer looked down at his report again. "Says here that your wife left yesterday at 2:00 p.m. to go shopping in town. You expected her back in approximately an hour. When she didn't come home, you made your first call to her cell phone at 3:30 p.m., and there was no answer. Does that sound right?" The officer hesitated before raising his eyes toward John.

The devastated husband nodded. "Yeah."

"She's twenty-five. You remember her wearing a blue hoodie and jeans? The picture you gave me shows a woman holding a baby. You said she's driving a blue, 1998 Pontiac Firebird." Officer Goseyun read the words from the document in an emotionless voice and then looked up at John.

A round wooden clock ticked off the seconds on a wall behind the desk. A phone rang behind a closed door. The odors of stale coffee and ashtrays piled high with cigarette butts on vacant desks in the room added to John's sense of desperation.

"Anything come to you after you left here?"

"I called her mother. I thought about her car, it could have broken down. It's old and needs new tires. A few other things, too. She'd call there for help." He cleared his throat and continued. "She isn't there. Her mother said she never called yesterday."

"Why wouldn't your wife call home for help?" Officer Goseyun placed a hand on the report and looked into the eyes of the husband across the desk.

"Okay, we fought before she left." A red patch climbed up his neck to cover his face. "I wanted to go meet some guys for a bike run. She didn't want to bring the baby shopping with her. Anne was hot to the touch yesterday morning. Rose said she needed to stay home. I yelled." His hand made a fist on top of the table.

"Do you fight often, John?" Officer Goseyun pushed the report to the side of his desk. He pulled out a yellow pad from his desk drawer and reached for a pen.

"I didn't hit her, if that's what you're thinking. We had a fight. Married people fight. I love my wife." John put his hands on the desk and pushed himself upright. "I'm done here. My daughter is with my sister. I'm going home. Are you gonna do anything to find her?"

Officer Goseyun stood. "I'll put an APB out for your wife's car. But you know we have hundreds of miles of roads here in Arizona. It'll take time." The officer reached out to clasp John's hand. "Go home, take care of your daughter. We'll do what we can here. I'll be in touch."

Officer Goseyun walked with John Tessay to the door of the police station. When he returned to his desk, he made a note on the report. *Husband fought with wife. Showed aggressive behavior.* He opened a drawer and took out the only file he kept there. Police reports of dozens of missing girls and women. After he read each heartache again, he placed the recent addition on top. Sorrow edged lines on his face. Would they find this one?

~~~~~

MISSING. The flyer pinned to the bulletin board had yellowed with age. Open to the fickle weather of rain, snow and sweltering heat, it took on its own identity of tragedy in front of the Lakota Sioux reservation's tribal offices.

"Walter, she's only fifteen." The white-haired woman turned to her husband. Her hand pushed the paper flat so she could read the message.

"Pretty, too. There's more like that one, Gertie, under hers." Her husband moved the edge of the poster over to show others tacked, one on top of the other. Dates and faces changed, but they all said essentially the same thing.

MISSING: a name, a picture, and what she was wearing when last seen. The dates ended with 2018, 2017, 2017, 2016. They all said, "If you have any information, contact the South Dakota State Police," and gave a phone number.

A bulging cloth shopping bag in his wife's hands prevented her from getting to her eyeglasses. She leaned in close to the poster to read. Her nose almost touched the paper.

"Where do you think she went? And the others? They're all young girls, too young to be living alone, away from family."

The girl in the photo drew Gertie Feldman to her. She had a granddaughter of the same age, involved in after-school activities back home in Brooklyn, New York. Gertie accompanied her to the school basketball games.

"Theresa is fifteen, and I can't imagine her living alone. The only meal she knows how to make for herself is breakfast. A box of cereal. There're basketball hoops on the sides of buildings, so it looks like they play some sports."

Gertie stepped back from the bulletin board. "Their mothers must be terrified, wondering what happened to their daughters. What happens after the posters are put here? I want to know more. When we get back to the hotel tonight, I'm going to ask our guide."

"There isn't much here for young people. Look at the other notices. Mobile homes for sale. The pictures show they're old, in need of repair. People looking for work put up cards with names and phone numbers." Walter pointed to one. "This one says, 'Will do anything.' It sounds desperate."

"I read the books the Elderhostel tour guide suggested and listened to the lectures, but I'm not prepared for this. Our trips to the southwest show me a different life than what we have at home. The Lakota lecturer told us how unemployment is as high as 80% to 90%. Families have become despondent. He said that the ugly truth is there is child molestation within families. He also said how difficult it is to live miles away from schools. Children still have to go to boarding schools 50 to 60 miles away from their families for an education. The young people aren't taught their tribal traditions. They don't have respect. Thousands of missing girl's reports are made yearly. Little news makes its way off reservations."

She looked down the street at the rundown homes, old trailers and small houses made from scraps of found material. The face of poverty. Vegetable gardens grew in front yards. A small boy played ball with a small dog of no distinct parentage.

There were lots of mongrel dogs on the reservation, and they all looked alike. When the tour bus stopped at gas stations or cafes, skinny dogs congregated, hoping for a handout. Their driver bought hot dogs to feed the strays.

"When we rode the tour bus across the reservation, I saw grass as far as the horizon. The mountains in the back appear strong and protective. The country looks beautiful and peaceful. Everyone's been friendly. It seems to be a nice place to live, but the lecturer last night said there's little medical care and the life expectancy average is fifty-five." She turned to Walter. "I wonder where the girls go, or how? They're too young to have cars." Gertie shivered. "There's a chill in the air."

Walter looked down at the road the tour bus had traveled on all morning. "They hitchhike Gertie, remember seeing the young people along the road with their thumbs out today? They'll do anything to get away."

After one last glance at the girl's picture on the poster, the couple turned to leave.

A sudden gust of wind blew across the bulletin board and raised the poster. The girl's eyes followed the couple. She seemed to cry out, PLEASE, SEE ME.

CHAPTER ONE

"Mom! Chooli's gone. She disappeared from the Cottonwood Mall."

Sally Li listened to her daughter's hysterical words on the phone, but couldn't believe what she'd just heard. Her granddaughter was missing.

"Grace, slow down, take a breath and tell me what happened." A pain pierced Sally's head. She closed her eyes, listening to her own heavy breaths as her daughter's voice caught with a sob and then continued.

"She was at the mall with three other girls shopping for prom dresses. The mother of one of the girls dropped them off. There was a meetup time at noon for lunch. The other girls showed up, but Chooli didn't. They looked all over the mall. Had her paged on the loudspeakers. Mall staff searched the rest-rooms and the food court. Shop managers combed their stores. She's not there." Grace gathered another breath, and said. "Chooli's a level-headed teenager. I trust her. She wouldn't go off on her own without telling someone." A heart-breaking sob traveled across the miles between Grace Begay on the Navajo reservation and Sally in Albuquerque. "I called her cell phone. No answer." In a weak voice, Grace added, "I'm afraid something's happened to her."

Sally took a deep breath. Her daughter was strong, a lawyer for the Navajo Nation. She had lived on her own off the reservation while she completed law school. The helpless message was so unlike her. "I'm coming to get you. It's 1:15 now, I'll be there by 2:30. Is Paul home?"

"No, I called him, he's on his way. But shouldn't I stay here? In case Chooli calls."

"I don't want you to be alone. You can transfer calls to my phone. We'll decide when I get there."

"You have a connection with her, Mom, do you sense anything? Can you see her?" There was hope in Grace's voice.

"She's alive, Grace. We'll find her." Sally put the phone down, wrinkled her forehead and stared at her granddaughter's picture on her desk. Chooli's golden brown eyes mimicked hers. She looked more Anglo than Navajo with her soft brown hair that tended toward curls. Sally kept her curls the golden blond they had been when she was younger. The picture next to Chooli was of her daughter, Grace, in a traditional Diné ribbon dress. Grace had inherited her Navajo father's dark eyes and straight black hair. Sally sighed and whispered, "Where are you, Chooli?"

The first time Sally noticed a psychic connection with Chooli had been a surprise to both of them. She was sitting in a rocking chair Grace gave her on her Albuquerque condo move-in day. A pain suddenly ripped across the back of her head, and she dropped the book she was reading. She rubbed her head and sensed her granddaughter's presence. She knew Chooli was hurt.

Sally immediately placed a call to Chooli's cellphone and learned her granddaughter had been hit hard in her head during a basketball practice session at school.

"Grandma, I'm okay, but after the ball hit me, your face came to me. You looked worried."

So it had happened again. Since childhood, Sally occasionally received messages from people at a distance from her. She discovered years ago that she could see her mother's worried face when she wasn't home from school on time. Or when she was out late on a date. She hated it back then. But that was years ago, and she had learned the messages could be important, so now she listened for them.

There were times when Chooli's angry words shouted into the wind while riding her horse, came to her. "Why does he have to drink? I hate him, I hate how he hits mom when he's drunk." Her father had come home drunk again. The teenager wondered where he got the booze and why did he have to drink? "I have to go to school and follow rules. He needs to stop drinking."

Chooli got into trouble at school when her classmates were making fun of her for looking Anglo. She did the best she could to straighten her curls before school, but by the end of day she had curls again. She shouted at them, "I'm Navajo, same as you." When Sally heard her granddaughter's cry, she vowed to teach the child to be proud of her dual ancestry.

Her special relationship with Chooli began while she was teaching school in China. Three years ago, Sally left her home on Cape Cod to go on a backpacking trip with a girlfriend to China. Both women had turned sixty-two and retired from teaching. On her first day in Shanghai, she found herself in People's Park watching a handsome, older Chinese gentleman practice Tai Chi. After he noticed her clumsy attempts to follow his movements, he introduced himself as Han Li and told her he taught English to Chinese students. A friendship between them began that day as Sally said, "I tried to learn Mandarin before I came here. But it's too complicated for me."

He laughed at her. "How about the fact that you have many words with the same meaning, and some words sound the same but are spelled different? Would you like to come visit my class and speak English?"

They went to his school, and then on a date to a park in Shanghai. As Sally traveled across China, Han kept in touch by phone. While in Yangzhou, she spent two days with his students and found them eager to speak English with her. Her visit to China ended after a romantic evening with Han on her last night in Yangzhou.

Sally returned to her home on Cape Cod. Four months later, a letter came from the Yangzhou school's principal offering her a position teaching spoken English at his school. An apartment and stipend were included in the contract. Her suitcase was barely unpacked. Her turnaround time back to China was severely hampered by the country's laws. But when she arrived, Han was there to greet her. He transferred his teaching job to her school, and they quickly became inseparable. Han's dreamy proposal resulted in a Chinese wedding.

Her new-found pleasurable life in China was upended one day when a mysterious envelope arrived, postmarked from Gallup, New Mexico, USA. The letter began, "Hi, Grandmother."

~~~~~

Forty-three years earlier, seventeen-year-old Sally left her parent's home in Boston, Massachusetts, after graduation from high school. She enrolled as an art student at the University of New Mexico in Albuquerque, over two-thousand miles from everything she knew. New Mexico quickly captured her heart. The stars in midnight black skies sparkled a welcome, cactus flowers added delicate pastel colors to green foliage, teenagers smiled and welcomed her to Albuquerque.

One day when she was reading under a tree on the campus lawn, a book suddenly fell at her feet with a thud. When she looked up, a Navajo boy stood in front of her. He bent down to pick up the book as she started to rise. Their heads connected. She fell back down. "Ouch, you have a hard head."

"I'm sorry." He reached down to help her up. "Hi, I'm Atza. You're new here."

"My name's Sally and I'm from Boston. I just got here a week ago. How did you know I was new?"

"Few students here with blond curls. You're beautiful. Let me show you around." He kept hold of her hand after she stood. She gazed into the most beautiful dark eyes she had ever seen and kept a firm hold on his hand. By the time the afternoon campus tour ended, the two had discovered they were destined for each other.

Their love story was marred when Atza took her to meet his mother. She took one look at Sally's blond curls and white skin and turned her back to the couple. "You cannot be with this girl. She's Anglo. Too much trouble for you. You need a good Navajo girl for a wife. If you marry this girl, she will not be accepted by the Navajo, your children will not be accepted by Navajo." But when the seventeen-year-olds learned that Sally was pregnant, they snuck away and were married by a Justice of the Peace in Arizona.

Shortly after, Atza left school and joined the Army to support his new family. When Sally was six months pregnant, he was sent to Vietnam. She moved in with his mother and tried to learn how to be a Navajo, but in her mother-in-law's eyes, failed at everything she did.

A week before her baby girl was born, a letter arrived from the Army saying Atza had been killed in action in Vietnam. Sally tried to care for her baby, but she fell into a deep postpartum depression. Atza's mother cared for baby Grace and loved her with an intensity that replaced her lost son. Teenage Sally spent days in her bedroom, unable to reach out to the baby that reminded her of her lost husband. Grace's cries brought excruciating pain. When Atza's mother said she wanted to adopt Grace, Sally agreed. Her daughter would have a traditional Navajo upbringing. Adoption papers were signed with the stipulation that Sally would not try to contact her daughter.

When Sally placed her daughter in the child's grandmother's arms, she felt a pain in her heart as she turned to leave. She returned to Boston and eventually finished her schooling there to become a teacher. Southwest colors crept into her household furnishings. Although she could not bring herself to return to New Mexico, a longing to know what happened to her daughter stole into Sally's dreams.

~~~~~

The letter that began, "Hi, Grandmother" was written by Grace's thirteen-year-old daughter. It revealed that Atza did not die in Vietnam but had been held captive in a Hanoi prison. He had returned to Albuquerque after the war and lived with his mother on the rez, helping to raise his daughter. When he became sick, his granddaughter used a computer search to trace Sally to Cape Cod, where a friend gave Chooli her grandmother's address in China.

After that first breakthrough, a close relationship with Chooli developed in an exchange of letters. Each shared their lives at home, their hopes and dreams. Their flourishing relationship motivated Sally to move to Albuquerque, New Mexico, to reunite with her Navajo family. The University of New Mexico offered Han a job teaching China history and Mandarin to their students.

When Sally arrived in the Albuquerque airport, Chooli flew into her arms. "Grandma!" Sally's arms wrapped around the teenager in a tight embrace. When she looked over her granddaughter's shoulder at her daughter for the first time in over forty years, Sally's heart erupted into a staccato rhythm. Tears flooded her eyes. Grace, her daughter, in front of her ter a lifetime apart. A beautiful woman dressed in traditional Navajo attire stood back as she watched her child's joyful union with her grandmother.

Grace glared at her mother, her lips in a tight line. "You abandoned me. I never had a mother."

"I'm sorry, Grace, I always loved you. Someday, I hope you can forgive me."

It took many months for the two to take tentative steps toward establishing a close relationship.

~~~~~

The back door to the condo squeaked as Sally closed it behind her. Her husband, Han, was practicing Tai Chi under their summer arbor. His shadow patterns moved across the flagstone patio. Water from their garden fountain cascaded down a rock shelf. In a pool at the bottom, chickadee birds splashed, their tiny feathers reflecting a kaleidoscope of colors.

He stopped as she came close. Han held out his arms and enfolded her into a tight embrace.

"What's wrong? You're shaking."

"It's Chooli. Grace called. Chooli's missing. Something happened at the Cottonwood Mall today. She was supposed to meet friends for lunch and didn't show. They searched everywhere for her. Grace is beside herself. I need to get her and bring her here."

"Wait. Don't you think we should wait for more news? Maybe Chooli left the mall to go somewhere and forgot the time."

Sally shook her head, "Something bad has happened. I have bumps up and down my arm. I can feel fear. I'm sure it's coming from Chooli. I saw her face for a moment while I was reading." She held out her arm to Han. "Look, I'm even getting red blotches. We don't have time to waste. Grace is frightened. I need to get to her. I can't abandon her again. She needs me."

"Okay, we'll go. But what about Chau and his computer friends? It's possible they can help find Chooli."

"You're right. I'll send him a message." She stopped her dash for the door and sat down at her laptop. Several deep breaths later, she closed the lid and stood up. "There, it's done. I told him we needed help to find Chooli. That we're on our way to get Grace, it'll be at least three or four hours before we're back, and the door key is under the mat." She got up from her desk and headed for the door.

"Wait." Han returned to the kitchen.

Sally had the engine running and the air conditioner on when Han opened the car door. "I have water bottles and a bag of chocolate chip cookies. We can go. You shouldn't drive while you're shaking. I'll drive."

"No, you can't drive. You're not a safe driver."

"I have a New Mexico driver's license. I am safe." His eyes held hers.

Her arms crossed across her chest, she took deep breaths, waiting. Minutes passed. Finally, she lowered her eyes first.

"Alright, you can come with me, but I'm driving. You drive a car like a moped in China. The wrong side of the road in traffic, and fifty miles an hour on the highway. I need to get to Grace fast. Hurry, get in the car."

CHAPTER TWO

Sally left the security of Mesa Village and their condo on Lester Drive behind. She turned onto Constitution Avenue, Wyoming Boulevard, then Interstate 40, and joined the hundreds of delivery trucks barreling along at over 80 miles an hour. The sun's golden rays bounced off hot steel trailer beds. She reached above the visor for her sunglasses, gripping the steering wheel so hard her knuckles turned white. "I'll never get used to these trucks racing faster than the speed limit. It's wall-to-wall trucks on the blistering hot pavement."

Han said, "Talk to me. Tell me about Chooli."

"She's smart. Her family history essay won the first-place award. Goes backpacking with Scouts. Is friendly to tourists, explains her Navajo culture." A glance at Han. "The news of hundreds of missing girls in New Mexico can't all be true. Some of them must come home."

Han reached over to squeeze her right hand. "You saw her face earlier. You always say that you have a connection with your granddaughter. We'll get her back."

Sally continued to murmur to herself as she watched the highway ahead.

~~~~~

Han sat silently next to her. His thoughts went back to a recent conversation at school.

A nervous student approached him. "I heard there's a girl missing from our school in Gallup. Girls disappear in New Mexico and never come back. No one does anything to stop it. What can we do to protect ourselves, Mr. Li? Can you teach us Tai Chi?"

He didn't have an appropriate answer for her. "It takes years to learn Tai Chi Chuan. The school officials say students should always travel in groups. There's protection when you're with others. Ask a friend to walk with you, or a school guard. Don't go out alone."

"My mother's worried. Girls are missing, and nobody is doing anything about it. She wants me to quit school, Mr. Li, and stay home. I don't want to leave school."

He turned to look at his wife. She was scared. What could he do to help her?

~~~~~

Sally left the highway in Gallup at the two-lane rez Route 491 and drove north on a series of dirt roads to Grace's trailer. Sally parked next to a car in the front yard. Swallowed some water from the bottle Han placed in her hand and opened the car door.

As she walked across the front yard, chickens scattered. Their flailing feathers raised small dust clouds. No one answered when she knocked and called, "Hello." She opened the door and stepped into a bare living room. Mail was scattered on a glass-topped coffee table. Under the glass were silver belt buckles that her son-in-law had won during his rodeo riding days. On the wall behind the sofa and table, Grace's framed diploma from law school hung along with Chooli's special awards.

Sally called, "Grace?"

Silence. The home appeared lifeless. Without familiar cooking odors, or family voices, an atmosphere of sorrow existed within the trailer. Sally moved from the living room, peeked into an empty kitchen, walked down the hall, and found her daughter in Chooli's room. Grace sat on the floor, scrunched in a corner, hugging a brown teddy bear. Tears ran down her face. She looked up at her mother and whispered, "I have to find her. She must be scared."

"The Ancestors will protect and care for Chooli." Sally trusted her daughter's powerful Navajo belief in their Ancestors to bring her comfort. She walked across the room and sat down next to Grace. Their shoulders touched. Sally bent her head. Her blond curls wrapped around Grace's straight black hair as they took comfort in each other's presence.

"We will bring her back." There would be time enough later for Sally to speak of her vision.

Silence descended as each woman looked around. Each relived memories of Chooli at her desk chewing a pencil as she studied for a school exam. Her moccasin toe taps as she practiced a Navajo dance step. Asleep in her bed, arms wrapped around her teddy bear.

When their private time with Chooli ended, Sally reached out her hand. "Come, we'll go into town. There's work for us to do there. Han is outside. Have you heard from Paul?"

"Paul came home about an hour ago. He didn't believe Chooli was missing. He called her cell phone. When she didn't answer, he became agitated and walked around outside, calling for her. He came back inside and said, 'I'll get help to find her.' He pulled his cell phone out from his pants pocket and punched in some numbers, nodded and smiled." Grace looked at the front door. "After he put the phone back, he ran for the door and called, 'You stay here, I'll be back.' He took off in the truck before I could tell him you were coming. I don't know where he is."

Sally called into the living room for Han. When he appeared at the bedroom door, she told him, "I want to bring Grace back to Albuquerque. Will you wait here for Paul and go back to Albuquerque with him?"

"I'll stay here. And wait for Paul." He held a bag of chocolate chip cookies in his hand.

"He may not come back. Here, take my car keys." Grace stood on wobbly legs.

When Sally could unbend her body and stand, a sparkle of light from Chooli's bedside table caught her eye. Her granddaughter always wore the silver bear necklace lying there. A birthday gift from Sally. When she reached for the necklace, she saw the broken clasp. After dropping it into her pocket, she helped Grace pack an overnight bag, and the two left the trailer.

Sally ushered her daughter into her car, started the engine, and said to Grace, "I sent Chau a message before I left home. He and his university friends can search the internet. They may be at the condo when we get there."

~~~~~

Sally had met Chau on her flight from Beijing to Albuquerque the previous year, when the teenager sat next to her.

"Are you going home to America?" He asked. "I have school in Albuquerque."

She looked into dark eyes and the smiling face of a handsome young man who clearly wanted to talk. "I'm going to Albuquerque to meet my daughter and granddaughter."

"I'm afraid I do not have good enough English. This is my first trip away from China." He looked down at his tightly clasped hands.

"I'm afraid, too. I've not seen my daughter for many years. My granddaughter is a teenager, and this will be the first time I see her. The University of New Mexico is an excellent school. The students are friendly, you'll fit in. What subject are you studying?"

"I come for art. There is good art in New Mexico. I want to use my computer for art studies."

Before the plane landed, Sally and Chau exchanged cell phone numbers, and when they disembarked the plane Sally pointed to a group of teenagers jumping up and down and waving a sign, *Welcome Chau*!

"There are your people. Go."

He took a step forward and then stopped. "Call me, please."

~~~~~

Chooli's letters had told Sally that her grandfather, Atza, had cancer and wanted to see Sally one more time. When she arrived in Albuquerque, she discovered her first love was dying. They spent days together reminiscing about their past. One afternoon, Atza's eyes roamed the sky. "My time here ends soon. You've brought me great happiness."

She asked him, "What can I do for you?"

"You are all I need." After more minutes of searching the clouds, a strangled breath, and, "I wish I could see my friends again. We were family in Hanoi. I wish I could say goodbye."

Sally used the cell phone number Chau gave her to make a request. "Is it possible to find POWs on the computer?"

Chau and his friends used their computer savvy to negotiate a reunion of Vietnam prisoners of war. Cellmates in the Hoa La Prison in Hanoi, the prisoners had developed communication among themselves by using a tap code to keep up their morale. The code was used to endure years of pain and loneliness. The POW's had scattered across the United States after their return.

When the computer kids located the old soldiers, they set up a meeting for them to be together on screens hung at the University of New Mexico's gym. College students in each POW's home town set up cameras and screens so the men could view and talk to each other for a heartwarming reunion.

~~~~~

The engine started with a rumble. Sally backed the car around and stopped to wave to Han. He stood in the doorway and waved back. She thought how he was always there when she needed him and wondered what was going to happen.

. She pulled onto the road. "Did you call Ann?" Sally looked at her daughter's frozen face. Grace needed the understanding of a lifelong friendship. As her mother Sally could nurture Grace, but Ann Yazzie would supply the support Grace needed to move forward. They had become "blood sisters" after a fight in Grammar School. Ann had teased Grace for being half-Anglo, and Grace hit her. Grace apologized, and they mixed blood from their wounds to form a blood-sister bond that lasted a lifetime.

"No, nobody." Grace clung to Chooli's teddy bear.

Sally pulled the car off the road and reached for Grace. "Give me your cell phone. I'll call Ann."

She kept the explanation of Chooli's disappearance brief. "I'm bringing Grace home with me." After turning her head away from her daughter, she whispered, "She's overwhelmed, not talking, and not prepared for what lay ahead. She needs you. Can you come to my condo in Albuquerque?"

Ann replied, "I'm on my way. I'll call for someone to take care of their chickens."

Back on the road, Sally listened to her daughter's shallow breaths. Tears ran unchecked down her face as her chest rose and fell in shallow gasps. Sally feared Grace would faint from the loss of air. She needed to talk.

Searching her memory for something to draw her daughter out, Sally asked, "Tell me again how Chooli fell off her horse the first time she tried barrel racing."

Grace turned tear-filled eyes toward her. "She was twelve. Her horse was big and fast. When they went around the last barrel, she cut it too close and leaned sideways to keep the horse from going down, and she slid off." Grace shook her head, as if to clear cobwebs.

"The horse fell on her. She pulled herself clear and stood up. She smiled and waved her hat to show she was okay. I was angry, scared, and proud of her all at the same time." She turned to her mother. "Do you know something?"

Sally didn't know how much to tell her daughter. She didn't feel comfortable sharing the little news that she was sure came from Chooli. "She's waving her hat now. I can sense her. Tell me more, I missed her childhood." Sally concentrated on driving the long Navajo Nation Route 9 toward Albuquerque. Her daughter was talking. Words spilling from her mouth kept fear from building up inside her head.

"She used to go to the ancient ruins with Father. They had a special bond. She told me Father was teaching her to hear the Ancestors' words on the wind." Grace was silent as the car moved across Navajo land. Barbed wire fences separated the road from the open prairie. White clouds hung low in the blue sky. The land seemed at peace. Sally's hands clenched the steering wheel. How could there be evil in this beautiful country?

Grace turned toward her mother. "I tried to learn from the Ancestor's, but I only felt the wind. I was cold in the ruins. The lost history scared me. Not Chooli. She belonged there." My father taught her the Navajo way. He wasn't there for me. He returned from Vietnam in 1971. I no longer was a child. I spent my early years without a father or a mother. Grace lapsed into silence again.

Sally reached across the seat and held her daughter's hand. "I believe your father is with her now. He was so strong in life. I'm sure his spirit can reach out to her."

~~~~~

It was 5 p.m. when Sally pulled into the condo complex where she lived with Han, a small community of university professors and retirees. The neighborhood had been recommended to Han when he began his teaching job at the University where Mandarin and Chinese history were part of a new curriculum.

He had married Sally and moved from Yangzhou, China. The close-knit, quiet neighborhood was an enormous cultural change for Han, but a welcome opportunity for Sally to be near her Navajo family.

The neighborhood was not quiet today. Cars moved up and down the street in front of their condo. College students handed out flyers. Sally stopped the car and watched as a car pulled in front of her condo to drop off more students and left with passengers carrying armloads of paper.

A familiar student spied Sally's car and waved for her to pull into an open spot in front of the condo.

"Where did they all come from?" Grace asked.

"I messaged Chau where to find a key and to go in if they needed a meeting place. I knew the trip across the rez would take hours. Students and neighbors are there. Are you okay with a crowd now? I can drive around the back and we can cut across the backyards."

"I'm alright. They're here to help. I want to tell them how much I appreciate this." Grace pasted on a brave face and took control of the moment as she reached for the door handle.

Red-headed Melinda was Chau's second-in-command and the first to approach the car. She had come from Ireland and started school the same semester that Chau started after arriving from China. They both found New Mexico strange at first and spent many hours together studying computer science, the one subject that had a universal history.

Melinda opened the car door. "We made up missing girl flyers with the picture of Chooli from your computer desktop. Everyone is using their printers to copy it and we're going out to post them. We plan to have Albuquerque covered and then move on to Grants. The school's branch in Gallup has already posted flyers on bulletin boards."

"Come on, we've something to show you inside." Melinda pulled at Sally's arm. She stopped to look at Grace. "We'll get her back. Everyone's helping."

Chau opened the front door and barreled down the walk. "Come in!"

Her living room had four laptop computers set up on tables, with young people intent on the screens. Printers dropped posters with Chooli's cheerful face on trays. Sally peeked at the computers as she walked past various views of mall shoppers.

"We got the security camera's footage from the mall and parking lot." Chau waved at the seated students.

Sally looked around, "That's great, Chau, but how did you get the tapes so fast? Don't you have to get permission?"

A teenager looked up at her. His dark Navajo eyes squinted for a moment and then he smiled. "You're not real computer savvy, Mrs. Li. Best stay that way."

"You mean you hacked . . .?"

Four sets of eyes stared at her. "You're right. I know little about computers. I'll make coffee." Sally turned to leave the living room.

Chau followed her into the kitchen. "The kidnappers don't want publicity. They want to stay under the radar. We plan to make that very difficult for them. News of a missing Navajo girl is being posted all over the internet. Her picture is on Facebook. Chat rooms are talking."

Grace stared at the computer screens. "I want to help."

The Navajo teenager stood. A traditional leather medicine pouch hung around his neck. A silver and turquoise cuff bracelet on his left wrist gave him a traditional Navajo presence. "Hello, my name is Randy. Come with me. We have a prayer circle next door. They need you." He held out his hand.

CHAPTER THREE

After leaving Grace at the neighbor's home, Randy joined Sally in the kitchen. "The women are performing a Navajo sing next door. Chooli's mother is in a good place."

Sally glanced at the teenagers staring at computer screens in the living room. They constantly updated each other with their findings. Chau said, "I have Chooli in front of a drugstore."

Melina spoke up. "She's looking at shoes." A voice from across the room said, "She's with a threesome of teenagers near an exit."

Sally put a kettle on the stove to make tea, but the rumble of voices from the front room intensified. She put her hand on her forehead. The chatter in the front room felt like a sledgehammer beating on her brain.

She turned off the stove and removed the kettle. Then stepped back into the living room and touched Chau's shoulder to draw him away from his computer screen. "I need to go to my bedroom and lie down. I'm getting a horrible headache." With one last glance around at the dedicated kids immersed in their enormous undertaking, she left the room and its chaos behind.

She loved how her bedroom reflected the serene southwest landscape. A green cactus with bright purple flowers in a clay pot brought the outside in. On the wall behind her bed hung a painting of Monument Valley's beautiful red rocks that she had bought on a recent trip there with Han. A Pendleton blanket covered her bed. Bedroom bliss eased her tension as she pulled window shades to block out sunlight, kicked off her shoes, and crawled into bed. Pressing the "on" button for her music player brought gentle Navajo flute music through ear pads.

A vision she had seen earlier bothered her. Minutes before Grace's call to tell her Chooli was missing, an image of Chooli had appeared on the page of the book she was reading.

The words blurred on the page, then disappeared, and her granddaughter's face appeared. The fear in Chooli's eyes caused a jolt of panic to course through Sally's body. Then Chooli's image disappeared.

Using Tai Chi breathing exercises she had learned in China to relieve her migraines, Sally lay on her bed with her hands covering her stomach. She breathed in through her nose and felt her stomach expand, then blew the air out through her mouth. After four breaths, she relaxed and drifted off to sleep.

Soft Navajo drumbeats joined the flute. The rhythm changed from a slow meandering to a faster tempo. The heartbeat of the drums matched hers. The drum beat lured her away from the peaceful flute notes as its rhythm sped to an electric crescendo. A flash of golden light and Chooli's face appeared. Sally called out to her. She willed herself to see more. She saw a wheelchair. Chooli's head bent forward, her chin on her chest. A slight turn, dark hair parted to reveal eyes half shut. Her mouth hung open. Her chest rose and fell in deep breaths. Sheet metal underneath the wheelchair bounced. Cardboard boxes off to the side. Someone sat next to her. A man held Chooli's arm. What was he doing? As Sally stared at her granddaughter in horror, Chooli called out, "Grandma, help!" Then nothing. The drumbeats disappeared, and only the flute music from her player remained.

Sally jumped up and raced into her living room. "I saw her!"

Chau met her at the open doorway. "We found her on the surveillance screens. They took her in a wheelchair. We're following it now. It looks like a man came in the front door pushing another man wrapped in blankets in a wheelchair. They walked through the mall several times, then it appears they chose Chooli and followed her. They stopped her close to a side entrance. Two men stood in front of the wheelchair talking, blocking the surveillance cameras from seeing what happened next. Then we see them pushing the wheelchair out the side entrance and Chooli disappears."

After seeing Sally's tears, he finished with sad eyes. "I'm sorry."

One of the seated computer experts added, "We're following the men who were talking when they grabbed Chooli around the mall, and looking for better facials of the kidnappers. They avoid the cameras. It looks like a well-planned grab-and-go. We still have footage of the parking lot to inspect."

"I think she was in some kind of truck or van." Sally looked at the screens. "I saw her in a wheelchair. There were boxes around her. It looked like the inside of a delivery van. She moved, but it didn't look like she was alert. Her eyes were half-shut."

Melinda had been outside, directing the coming and going of volunteers. She opened the front door. "A police car just pulled up. We should probably shut down the laptops. It may not be good for them to see our mall pictures." She called to Sally, "Mrs. Li, maybe you can talk to them. Chooli's mother is next door. They have a prayer vigil. Randy said it's best to leave her there for now. More families have joined them. They bring peace and hope to each other. Her friend, Ann, is with her."

Han entered behind Melinda and shouldered his way past the room's occupants. He carried two large bags that filled the room with the unmistakable aroma of Chinese takeout. "It's dinnertime. I called Golden Dragon for food to feed our helpers. I'll bring it into the kitchen. Everyone come and get some. There's cold soda, too." He disappeared behind the kitchen door. The kitchen counter quickly became a Chinese buffet with rice, vegetables, dumplings, and chicken wings.

Sally put her hand on his shoulder and whispered into his ear, "Thank you. I don't know what to do next. Police are outside, I have to talk to them."

He wrapped his arms around her. "Practice Qi Gong. Listen to your breaths. You can feel the air come in through your nose and hear it blow out through your mouth. It sounds like a summer breeze blowing through forest trees. First, you take small steps, one step makes room for more. An enormous project is soon complete."

Sally walked into the front room to meet the police as Grace's husband, Paul, limped into the room. After a rodeo fall, he was left with a stiff left leg. A round belly covered his belt. With him came a Navajo man with long gray hair caught in a ponytail down his back. Turquoise and silver necklaces hung over his suede shirt. Years of knowledge had etched deep lines on his face. He stopped for a moment, dark eyes scanned the room's occupants, then followed Paul into the kitchen. The students watched the newcomers as they crossed the living room to the kitchen.

Two uniformed Albuquerque police officers stood just inside the open front door, with Melinda. Four university students stood with closed laptop computers in their hands. Everyone was talking.

Chau made eye contact with his friends and three of them disappeared out the front door with Melinda. He assumed a casual stance with his back against the far wall, feet crossed in front; his hands held a closed laptop as he gazed at the police.

A now near-empty room left Sally with the police. She stood before them, wondering how they knew to come here. She didn't remember calling them, but someone must have. What did they know? She stepped forward. "Hello, I'm Sally Li. The missing Navajo girl is my granddaughter."

The younger officer showed her his badge. "We're from the Albuquerque PD. My name's Frank Milford. We got a call from the Cottonwood Mall office saying a young Navajo girl is missing. We interviewed a woman there who said she had brought teenage girls to the mall to shop for prom dresses. It looks like you're conducting a search for the girl. We found a poster at a Burger King outside the mall. We would like to get some information from you to help in our search."

Sally swiveled her head to look at each man. "Grace called me hours ago. Someone took my granddaughter at the mall today. Family and friends are here to help find her."

Warren Granger, the older officer, said, "We'll put out an APB notice to search. Is the picture of the girl on your posters recent?"

Sally nodded. "I took it last month on her birthday. Is that all you can do? The kidnappers could be anywhere." Sally knew her face was turning red as she squelched down the anger growing in her stomach.

"She might turn up. Sometimes young people decide to take off on their own, but return, or call, when they want to sleep in their own bed. It happens." The older officer stared at Sally; his body language stiff.

"The missing girl is my granddaughter. She didn't run away from home. Someone took her from the mall." Sally was about to say more about seeing Chooli in her dream, but she closed her mouth. Many times, in the past, people had ridiculed her when she spoke about the dreams she never wanted, the dreams that woke her in a panic.

The day little Bobby Evans disappeared, Sally heard him crying. She called the police station to tell them she knew where to find the little boy. Sally was fifteen then.

And had been Bobby's babysitter. The dream woke her with his calls for his mommy. He was in a wooded area in the town park, curled up beneath an oak tree. Police searched in the wrong place. Someone said they saw him on the other side of town. Sally remembered his parents' pleading for his return on television news. When a neighbor finally listened to Sally's directions and began a search in the park, he found the boy and brought him home. Bobby's parents were grateful. The police never acknowledged her part in the rescue.

Officer Milford stepped forward. "There's a lot of territory to cover. We'll have every officer in Albuquerque looking for your girl as soon as we can, and we'll alert the New Mexico State Police. I am sorry for your loss . . . that this happened. We'll do everything we can to find her." He shook his head. "What you're doing here is more than we can do with our limited workforce. I'll call if I have any news. We tried to get information from the mall's surveillance cameras, but it looks like they weren't working around the time she disappeared."

Sally glanced over at Chau. His mouth shut in a firm line. A miniscule shake of his head told her it wasn't them.

As the officers turned to leave, Warren Granger looked at the closed kitchen door. "If anyone can help, it will be Hosteen Begay. He's legendary."

After the police left, the students crowded back into the living room. Everyone was talking at once and shaking their heads. Chau looked at Sally. "We didn't scrub the cameras. The kidnappers did. We're dealing with sophisticated scum."

Melinda looked worried. "Everyone needs to be very careful from now on. If they used computers on the mall cameras, it may not take them long to be onto us."

"You should shut down the computers. I don't want you to be in danger." Sally stood in front of Chau. Her hands shook with nervous tremors.

"Does anyone want to quit?" Chau asked the computer experts. As an answer, they walked to the tables each had been using, sat down, and opened their laptops.

"I thank you. But please be careful. Don't use names or places they can trace back to you." Sally walked to each student to shake hands.

Chau looked up. "We'll be careful, but it's possible the kidnappers will discover your condo. No telling what kind of sophisticated equipment they have."

Han stepped in from the kitchen. "We must all be careful. Now is a good time to take care of ourselves with Chinese food. Take a rest and eat." He didn't need to repeat that request.

Sally dragged Han out the back door into the garden. "Chooli and the kidnappers could be anywhere. Don't the police read the newspaper? Girls are going missing all the time, no wonder they're not found, they could be on the other side of the world by the time the police decide to get involved. Chooli did not run away from home. Someone took her."

Han raised a hand to stop her. "The police said they were going to start work on the search right away. People are here to help. We're conducting our own search and rescue. The students don't need to see you losing control. Stay out here until you can come in and behave like an adult, not a child having a temper-tantrum." He opened the door to the kitchen and closed it behind him.

Sally watched his back disappear behind the closed door. "Han, I'm not a child. Chooli could be in pain. Every hour that goes by means she could be further away. We know someone took her." She paced over to the summer arbor and back. "I saw her in my dream, Chau found her on the computer screen. We need to go find her now." She stomped her foot and sat on the wood bench by their outdoor succulent garden.

Voices from the kitchen seeped under the door. "Chicken wings, my favorite . . . this is good fried rice." She heard Han give instructions on the use of Chinese chopsticks. The Golden Dragon chicken wings were her favorite. She stood and followed her nose into the kitchen. Han raised his head from behind a teenager. "You better hurry and fill your plate before it's gone."

With paper plates full of food, students sat in the living room discussing the merits of Chinese food vs cheeseburgers with green chili. An occasional glance at the animated computer screens showed information on missing and murdered girls and women. People in chat rooms were discussing the latest missing Navajo girl.

"I have something." A student put his plate down. "There's a note from a woman in New York. She and her husband were vacationing in South Dakota and saw a poster about a missing girl. They want to help. She identifies as

Gertie Feldman and says her husband, Walter, was in the furniture business before retiring. They have a database of businesses across the country and will send out a notice. She feels they have some clout." He pushed "print," and copied Gertie's message.

CHAPTER FOUR

Sally stood by the closed front door and asked, "What now?" The students had devoured their plates of Chinese food, made notes on their computers, and stood to leave. A chorus of "Thank you" followed grateful smiles before they left.

Chau's last words to her were, "We found excellent pictures of the men at the mall who blocked the camera when they took Chooli. We sent them out on computer websites. That will make the evil men very unhappy." He held Melinda's hand as they left. The contrast of his Chinese dark eyes and her green eyes and Irish-red hair turned heads when they were together in public. Sally thought that they made the joining of foreign cultures work.

Empty takeout containers littered the kitchen. Soda cans filled a waste container for recycling. The four remaining adults stared at the closed door as a weighty silence descended.

The Navajo Elder moved to stand in front of Sally. "You have seen Chooli." It wasn't a question.

"Yes, flashes. She calls for help."

"You have a spirit connection we can use to find her. Will you come to my medicine *hogan*? I have powerful energy there." The age lines on his face, a scar above his left eye, and intense dark eyes captured Sally. His powerful aura seemed to fill the room. She wondered who he was.

Paul said, "Hosteen Begay is my Great Uncle. He is a Navajo *hatalii*. I have seen him call on the Ancestors for help. The *Diné* recognize his wisdom and special abilities." He turned to Sally, his eyes brimming with tears. "He saw you with Chooli. He said you can find her."

Han pulled out a garbage bag from under the sink. He filled it with remnants of the Chinese buffet. "He's a wise man. I talked to him in the car on the way here. He's like my Qi Gong Master in Yangzhou. The Masters' study the human mind for many years, they learn how to see what we cannot. They listen to the wind and hear messages from our forefathers. I have seen them heal people and find lost treasures. He's an honorable man. You go with him."

"What do you have that's hers?" Hosteen asked. He looked around the front room. "A connection for you."

Sally opened her hand to show him the silver bear charm necklace. "This necklace. I gave it to her; she always wore it. She claimed it brought her good luck. It was on her bedside table. The chain has a broken clasp. I have a turquoise bear she gave me. We found the bears at a shop in Santa Fe last summer. Each of us saw our bear at the same time." She hooked her fingers inside her shirt and pulled out a small turquoise bear attached to a silver chain. "I wear mine all the time. We talked about our bears being symbols of powerful medicine."

"You can wear the bears together to join your spirits." Hosteen held out his hand for the necklaces. When Sally deposited them in his calloused hands, he took both bears off their silver chains and attached them to a leather thong he pulled from his pocket. He hung the thong around her neck.

Sally's legs shook as she moved across the room to her husband. Her body trembled so hard it quaked. "I apologize for my explosion out back. Chooli asks for my help to find her. I can feel her fear. Grace is beside herself with grief. I remember how I felt leaving her when she was a baby. It tore me apart, knowing I would never see her again."

Han bent so his lips touched her forehead. "You are forgiven. Go with Hosteen. We can trust this man. You will find her."

"Aren't you coming with us?"

He put his hands on her shoulders and gave her a gentle push toward Paul. "This is a time for family. You have a blood connection with Chooli and her parents. I might draw good energy away. I'll stay here and clean up." He held her shoulders and moved her away.

"It could be cold in my *hogan*. Do you have blankets to bring?" Hosteen stood at the door to the kitchen.

"I'll get some." Han returned with Sally's favorite Pendleton blanket and a green wool throw.

"Come, we'll go next door for Grace." Paul turned toward the door. His red eyes captured Sally's attention as he stepped toward her. "We will find her."

Green succulent plants with bright red flowers grew in a rock garden by the front door of the condo next door. A blue sky contrasted with the colors of the adobe house and garden. A drum beat floated on the air. As they drew closer, Sally could see inside the front room through the open door. Women sat on chairs in a circle, murmuring words to the beat of a small drum in the hands of a young girl. Her hair wrapped in a traditional bun behind her head and tied with white yarn, she sang in Navajo. She hit a round hand-held drum with a stick and tapped the rhythm with her other hand on her knee. When she saw Sally and Paul, she tilted her head to the side to direct the newcomers into the kitchen.

Grace was there with Ann, making sandwiches. "Have you heard something? Is it Chooli?" Seeing Paul and her mother, her hands shook and a sandwich hit the floor.

Sally answered, "No, nothing, I'm sorry. Hosteen Begay is here. He says I can find Chooli. We have a spirit connection. Come, we're going to his *hogan*."

Grace turned to Ann. "You come too."

Ann shook her head. "It's better I stay and help with feeding the *singers*. I'll be here when you return." Ann pulled Grace to her for a powerful hug. "Go with your husband."

Grace followed Paul to the car. "Do you know the way?"

"I've been there many times. After the bull crushed my leg in the rodeo accident, Hosteen made excellent medicine for me. The native herbs are better than Anglo drugs. He has native herbs to cure pain. Hosteen was taught by his father to know the words of the Plant People. The *Diné* go to him to perform the Blessing Way. It's known that he has found missing children. He's known on the rez as a healer with special abilities. When I went to his medicine *hogan*, he agreed to come with me to find Chooli." Paul opened the car's back door for Hosteen and Sally, then ushered his wife into the passenger's front seat. Before closing the door, he said, "I believe he can help your mother find Chooli for us."

~~~~~

The medicine *hogan* was over a two-hour drive from Albuquerque. Sally sat in the back seat with Hosteen Begay. His eyes were closed. He may be asleep, she thought, and used the opportunity to study him.

A ponytail of gray hair hung two feet down his back. Wisps of hair framed his face. Deep lines on his forehead and surrounding his eyes attested to years spent in the bright New Mexico sun. She wondered how he got the scar. His relaxed mouth still held a smile.

A three-by-four-inch deerskin bag hung around his neck. Sally had heard about such bags. Each one contained stones, corn dust, an animal fetish or other sacred items the wearer had collected during his life.

His shirt covered a lean chest. A belt with a silver buckle of a horse's head caught her eye. It was beautiful.

Her inspection finished, she laid her head back on the seat and closed her eyes. Her hand reached for the leather thong with the bears resting on her chest.

They arrived at the *hogan* after sunset. Stars filled the sky, sending enough light to see a trailer, the *hogan,* and pinon trees. Hosteen led them past a silver trailer and around a corral holding a dozen sheep. Next to the sheep corral, a Navajo weaving loom sat under a pinon tree with a completed wool rug a third of the way up from the bottom. Sally stopped to admire the rug. Hosteen joined her at the loom. "My wife enjoys weaving. I made her a strong loom for her to create beautiful rugs."

A metal design of a tree of life covered the front door. Sally stepped closer to admire the artwork. Next to the door, a leather dream catcher covered with eagle feathers hung in a window. As she leaned over to get a better view of the intricate webbing, a face flashed in the window. A woman stared at her from behind the window. Tears flowed down her cheeks. Startled, Sally opened her mouth to say something, but the face disappeared.

The rest of the group was standing in front of the *hogan,* and Paul waved at her to join them. She looked back at the window as she joined Hosteen's search party. Who did she see?

Inside the eight-sided log structure, bundles of dried herbs hung from tree branches set on tripods on one side of the single room. A cast-iron stove in the middle was cool to the touch. Beautiful Navajo rugs hung from the walls. Moonlight from a hole above the cook stove made patterns on the dirt floor as a gentle breeze blew from the open doorway, causing the herbs to sway.

Small woven blankets were scattered on the floor. Hosteen sat on a north facing square and motioned Sally to sit opposite him. After she was settled, Grace and Paul sat east and west, facing each other. Hosteen spoke in a deep, resonate voice. "We're in a sacred place. I'll call upon the Ancestors for help in finding Chooli. Her connection with her grandmother is strong." Sally reached for the bear charms. "You will go into a trance. Look for Chooli."

Paul held a drum and Grace lit a bundle of sage leaves to purify the air. She waved a feather over the bundle. Smoke rose in thin columns.

Hosteen closed his eyes and whispered.

Sitting with her legs crossed was difficult for Sally. She fidgeted during the prayers. Grace touched her arm and held out a pillow.

Sitting on the soft pillow was a blessing. After she closed her eyes, she smelled a tantalizing aroma from the hanging herbs. Their blend was something new. She relaxed and listened to the foreign words. It sounded like poetry spoken in a hypnotic rhythm.

She swayed to the drums' beat and listened to Hosteen. His words became softer, and the light in the *hogan* dimmed to a peaceful blue sky. A sweet scent separated from the herbs. The room became dark and a golden light flashed as other sounds intruded on the drumbeat. Someone was crying.

Intense heat from Chooli's silver bear suddenly caused Sally to drop her hand to her chest. From behind closed eyes, Sally heard her granddaughter's sobs.

When the beat of the drum ceased, Sally opened her eyes. The air in the room no longer held the sweet aroma from the herbs. Sally watched as Grace and Paul faded away. The sobs became louder, and then a desperate wail sounded, jarring Sally to search around her for the source. A chill crept up her back. The cold enveloped her in a cocoon. She was enclosed in a white fog that floated away as her eyes searched for the source of the crying.

She found herself in a cold, dark room. The sobs came from a figure crumpled up against a back wall. A ragged blanket did little to cover a bare body. The hair on Sally's arms stood straight up when she realized it was her granddaughter across the room. A woman to one side whispered to Chooli. Two more blanket-covered figures sprawled against a side wall.

Sally heard Chooli talking to the person next to her. Her breath caught in her throat and she moved from her cushion to approach her granddaughter. "Chooli, we will get you out. Are you hurt?"

Hosteen Begay's voice filled her head, loud and clear. "Do not touch her. If you touch her, you may not come back. You will stay there."

"But she needs comfort. There's pain all around me."

"Look around. Can you identify anything? What do you see?" The voice from the hogan stopped her.

"It's dark. There are four people here. I think they're all girls. There are bowls on the floor, looks like food. Taco Bell wrappers. Wait, the floor is dirt, the walls are stone. Maybe a cave. I smell body odor. People have been here for a long time."

Chooli moved to sit up and wrapped the blanket around her chest. Her face was red and tear stained, her hair hung in tangled clumps, and purple bruises covered her arms. "Grandmother, I hear you. Have you come for me? The men hurt me. I'm scared."

"Hosteen, Chooli's talking to me. She knows I'm here. How can I talk to her?"

"Hold the bears around your neck and speak to her. She will hear you."

Sally moved on her pillow and leaned toward Chooli. "We're looking for you Chooli. A healer sent me to find you. Do you know where you are?"

"A cave somewhere in Arizona, I think. Rose is with me. She remembers a long ride in the back of a van after two men grabbed her on her way home in Arizona. She was going home after shopping when a van passed her on the left on a deserted stretch of road and then halted in front of her. Two men jumped out of the van when she slammed on her brakes. The next thing she remembers is waking up in the van. She said she felt bumps from a dirt road. I think there are more caves here. I hear two men talking. Rose said she thinks she's been here for two days. We can't tell. It's always dark. It's awful here!" Chooli lapsed into tears. A scream. "Someone's coming."

Sally shook her head as she felt a pull from behind. "I want to stay with my granddaughter." Images of people in the cave disappeared, but she heard a man's voice. "I told you no talking, bitch." The sound of a slap. A cry of pain.

As the room disappeared, an image of brown leather boots with a carved bucking bronco on the sides remained.

Sally heard sobs from inside the *hogan* before she opened her eyes. Grace's face was covered with tears. She held a cup of water out to her mother to drink. Her hand shook, and drops fell over the side onto the floor. "You spoke to someone, do you remember? You became agitated, frightened, Hosteen pulled you back here."

"I saw Chooli. She's with others. In a cave somewhere, maybe Arizona. We must find them." Sally turned to Hosteen. "The last thing I saw were cowboy boots, and I heard a man's voice."

CHAPTER FIVE

Streaks of daylight fell through the smoke hole of the *hogan*. Dried medicine plant bundles hanging from the ceiling swayed as air blew in from the open doorway. Leaves rustled when neighboring creatures stirred. A distant call from a morning bird heralded a new day for the medicine *hogan's* sleeping foursome.

Sally opened her eyes and found herself under her Pendleton blanket. Her daughter moved toward her from the potbelly stove in the center of the *hogan,* a cup of tea cradled in her hands.

"Good morning, Mom. You drifted off after last night's trance and Hosteen said it was best to let you rest. Your connection with Chooli is strong. You crooned to her in your sleep. I think you both connected in a dream." Grace sat down next to her. "Are you alright? Hosteen is outside saying his morning prayers. We can go back to your condo when you're ready."

Sally discovered there was a Navajo rug underneath her and pillow type bedding under that. "Good morning, Grace.

How did I get on this bed? I slept with Chooli next to me. I sensed her breath on my face."

"Your eyes began to close, and you mumbled something. Hosteen brought the bed from the side of the *hogan*. You climbed onto it. I slept too. The herbs over our heads give out a comforting scent."

Sally struggled to release herself from the bed, sat upright and reached for the offered cup with both hands. She held it under her nose before taking a sip. "This is Navajo tea. I often drink it in the morning at home. I like its smokey taste, and this is even better with the honey. Thank you, Grace. I'm a little groggy this morning." She savored the familiar drink. Her brain was starting to clear when her son-in-law burst into the hogan.

His red face was wet with sweat, and he wheezed from exertion as he knelt by Sally and grabbed at her arm. "You're awake, I've been outside waiting."

She yelped. "Stop, you're hurting me."

He turned his gaze from her face to his hand. "Oh, sorry. Don't mean to hurt you." His fingers released her arm. "I gotta ask you. You told us last night you saw boots on one kidnapper. Were the toes pointed or rounded? Someone might know them." His intense eyes frightened her, and she pulled back.

"Don't move so fast," Grace said, as she reached for her husband's arm. "She's helping us. At least give her time to wake up."

"I don't know, Paul. I only saw them as the room faded." Sally lowered her eyes to escape his hard stare. "They were brown leather, with the image of a bucking bronco, scuffed and dirty."

"We can use the information to find Chooli." The anger in Paul's voice rose. "Someone knows who those boots belong to. I need to find them, stop the evil monsters from . . ." He rubbed the back of his head as he paced the confines of the *hogan.*

Grace spoke up. "Maybe she can find an image of similar boots on the computer. We should go back to Albuquerque."

Silence followed Paul's outburst. He shook his head and peered at Sally, then his wife. "I gotta do something. She's my daughter."

Sally stood and moved to the open doorway. "I hear Hosteen's voice. The words sound beautiful. I'm going to drink my tea outside." On the other side of the *hogan* door, a bright new day appeared. The sun rose over the distant pinon trees. Hosteen's words joined a chorus of morning birdsongs as the new day gave birth.

"Hózhóogo naasháa doo
Shitsijí' hózhóogo naasháa doo
Shikéédéé hózhóogo naasháa doo
Shideigi hózhóogo naasháa doo
T'áá altso shinaagóó hózhóogo naasháa doo
Hózhó náhásdlíí'
Hózhó náhásdlíí'
Yahweh náhásdlíí'
Hózhó náhásdlíí"

"In beauty, I walk
With beauty before me, I walk
With beauty behind me, I walk
With beauty above me, I walk
With beauty around me, I walk."

His words rang out across the prairie, first in Navajo and then English. After the prayer, he held out corn pollen dust to a breeze from the east and removed the deerskin medicine bag from his neck. He beckoned Sally to sit next to him on the rough-hewed log bench beside the door. "Come, sit, I have a gift for you." He held a small turquoise carving of a mountain lion in the palm of his hand. "Lion fetish will protect you."

She reached for it. Heat radiated from the stone as if it had been warmed by the sun. Her fingers wrapped around the smooth stone fetish, and she relaxed her shoulders. "Thank you. The beauty and confidence of the mountain lion has drawn me to them. I'm told they live within themselves."

"The spirit of the mountain lion will join with you. You can see the future with strong eyes." Hosteen studied her eyes for several moments and nodded.

Sally closed her fingers around the fetish in her hand. She allowed the warmth to seep into her chest. "Hosteen, why did you stop me from going to Chooli last night? She needs me. I could see her, hear her crying. I wanted to hold her. You said if I touched her, I might stay there. I don't understand."

He leaned forward. In a voice barely above a whisper, he began. "Years ago, my father taught me how to help a spirit find a lost loved one. Our family has used this ability for generations. We don't know why we have this gift, or why sometimes it doesn't work. My father told me the spirit must travel alone. And not to stay long. He warned me that sometimes the spirit does not return."

Hosteen looked down at the ground between his feet. "One time, years ago, a girl asked me to find her sister. They were twins. They had a close connection. I put her in a trance and saw her eyes search the surrounding space. Suddenly, she put her arms out and called her sister's name. Then she became still. She barely breathed. I pulled her out from the trance, but she was lost. She no longer talked. Her spirit was gone. I believe she reached out for her sister and their spirits became one. Her spirit is with her sister. I don't want that to happen to you." He reached for her hand. "That's why I gave you my lion fetish to protect you."

"Hosteen, I'll hold the lion while you bring me to Chooli." She started to say more, but Paul came charging out of the *hogan*. "Let's get to town. Maybe they have more information."

Chickens scattered as they left the *hogan*. The morning sun reflected off the trailer door. Sally slowed her steps as she walked past and glanced at the window. She looked for the dream catcher, but a shade covered the inside of the window. The room was dark. "Hosteen, I saw someone . . ." But when she saw his face, she didn't finish her sentence. Set in granite, his eyes flashed fire as he stared straight ahead, lips stretched tight. He quickened his steps past the trailer. Sally lowered her head and followed.

Everyone in the car wanted to talk to Sally, to ask questions. Her grip on the mountain lion tightened as her fear for Chooli in the hands of despicably evil men wracked her nerves. She answered as best she could, watched as Grace wrote in a notebook, and rubbed her forehead to avert a threatening headache. Time vanished as she closed her eyes to rest.

~~~~~

Han met the foursome at the condo's front door. His arms reached out to envelop Sally in a tight embrace. Air released from her lungs as she allowed herself to feel her husband's strength. She leaned into his arms and felt his gentle kiss on her forehead. "I was worried when you didn't come home last night. I called your cell, but it went to leave a message. Grace's friend, Ann, said you were safe with Hosteen. You can't go without me again." He looked over her head at Hosteen. "I go with my wife." He took her arm. "Come, you need sleep."

"I slept, Han. We were out of cell range. I nodded off in the car coming here and forgot to check my cell phone for messages." She rubbed her arm where he held her. "I'm tired of people yanking at my arm today. I saw Chooli."

A moment after he released her, she turned her head and saw distraught students in their front room. Their chatter had an intense energy stronger than yesterday. Half empty water bottles next to computer screens, work stations covered with crumpled tissues, gave the room a sad aura. Han moved in front to block her view of the students. Something was wrong.

"What happened? Why are they here? It's early." She pushed past him to be in front of Chau's screen. It showed a newspaper article titled, "*Another Lakota girl found dead.*"

Chau's eyes left the screen for a moment to look at Sally. "We're finding more missing and murdered girls throughout the southwest. The same age as us. The MMIW has identified murder as the third leading cause of death of indigenous women. It's not only about your granddaughter anymore. One of our family and friends could be next." He waved his arm around to show how close the threat was to each of them.

Melinda spoke up. "My friends at school are afraid to go anywhere. They don't feel safe. We found an article on the internet about two girls from South Dakota that were taken at gunpoint while hiking. One girl escaped, but the other is still missing. It's happening everywhere. No one's doing anything to stop it."

Randy entered the room and stood in front of Sally. "I took Chooli's mother next door. The ladies in the prayer circle have multiplied. Word has spread, and members of other missing girls' families have come here to support Grace and each other. There's strength and hope next door. We need to do our part here and help find Chooli. Someone out there has information for us."

He raised a fist in the air. Each of the other students rose from their workstations and followed suit. "We will succeed!"

Sally searched each eager face, wondering how could she tell the teenagers how special they were. "We learn hard truths in life. You're reading about one of the most heinous crimes committed to humankind. I heard of the disappearances before, but it happened to someone else. I never believed Chooli's name would be among the missing. We will get my granddaughter back, but my life will never be the same."

"All the more reason for us to find her." Chau huddled over his laptop. His fingers raced across the keyboard. "We're looking for patterns of where they disappeared and where bodies were found, clues on where to look for Chooli. The chat rooms are talking about the disappearance. People are asking questions. The statistics of thousands of missing person reports has come as a surprise to many white people. If the abductors lift their heads from their hole, we'll find them. Your husband is right, get rest. As soon as we have more information, we need to return to school." He turned back to the computer. "Dirty, rotten men, we'll get you," he muttered.

~~~~~

Han approached her from the kitchen. "Come have coffee and a sweet roll. You need to eat and then rest."

Sally sat at the kitchen table. "I'll have a lifetime to do that after we find Chooli." After a bite of the sweet roll, she licked her sugar-coated fingers. "Tastes good."

Paul called to her from the living room. "Can you look at this screen? She's got boots with a bucking bronco. See if you can find the one you saw."

Sally ran back to the living room. The screen was full of brown cowboy boots. "I can't tell," Sally said. "They look alike to me. The boots were dirty and scuffed. Must have been old." She turned to leave, but something caught her attention.

Leaning forward, she squinted at the screen and pointed to a pair of brown boots. "Those look familiar." Minutes passed before she looked up at Paul. "Except I think I saw them in a store last week when I was shopping. I'm sorry, I'm not much help."

Hosteen Begay was studying maps on Randy's laptop. "There are many caves in New Mexico and Arizona. We can eliminate the well-known ones. There's too much possibility of being found. She could even be in Colorado or further north. Alaska has lost thousands of Indigenous girls."

"I feel another headache coming." Sally clutched her head in both hands. "There's too much stress here. It's best I lie down." She dashed from the room, the intense pounding in her head a blinding pain.

The soft bed wrapped Sally in a warm embrace. She closed her eyes. Safe in her home, she wondered what more could there be in the cave. She had seen people, girls, and a man's scuffed brown boot. If only she could talk to them.

The bright light and dream came quickly.

It was dark in the cave. The girl Chooli called Rose pulled a blanket across her granddaughter's bare skin. The girl moaned. "I'm tired and cold."

"Your grandmother searches for you. She will come." Rose brushed her hand across Chooli's hair. She parted strands to reveal a tear-blotched face.

Chooli raised her head. "Grandma, I need you, they're horrible men, they said they're going to send me to Mexico."

Sally shivered. A mist of cold air from the cave settled at the foot of her bed. The slow progress of cold crept up her legs, and she reached for her blanket. How to reach Chooli? She was so close she could hear the girls' breath, their whispered words. What had Chooli said? If only she could talk to them. Who was the girl called Rose? She looked older.

Across the cave, two girls stirred. They reached for bottles of water. "Who are you?" one asked, "you're new."

"My name's Chooli. Men grabbed me at the Cottonwood Mall. I think I've been here a day. I can't tell, it's always dark. Where are we?"

"I think we're in Arizona," Rose said. "Two Anglo men stopped my car on my way home from shopping and put me in a van. I was almost home. I live in Arizona. My husband must be worried. We have a daughter. I wish I could tell him I'm alive. I don't remember being in the van long."

A girl from across the cave pulled dark hair away from her face and said, "I don't know how long I've been here. It feels like a long time. I was hitchhiking when a van stopped to pick me up. I was stupid. A guy said he'd give me a lift to Albuquerque. The rest I don't remember. They give us drugs and then touch us. They do more, but we need the drugs. Even when they hurt us, we want more drugs. I hear we're going to Mexico." She rubbed her right arm. Her voice cracked. "It'll be warm there. They're sending a truck for us."

"There've been more girls in this cave. You won't be here long." She waved her thumb at Chooli. "I've seen several

60

teenage girls like you here. Did they take your pictures yet? No one searches for runaway girls."

Chooli turned to look at the girl, at Rose. Her scream came from the bottom of her stomach. "I'm not a runaway. FIND ME!"

The urgent plea woke Sally. Hosteen sat in a chair next to her, while Han sat next to her on the other side of the bed. Hosteen said, "It's time for us to leave here."

"Where can we go? They could be anywhere." Sally got up and stood on shaky legs. "I had a dream. I saw her again. They're planning to move the girls."

"I heard you talking." He frowned. "If they move the girls now, their danger is greater. We must return to my *hogan*. I can help you locate the girls."

Sally went into the kitchen and opened the back door. "Why can't you put me in a trance here? I saw Chooli in a dream in my bedroom. It's so far to your *hogan* and takes a long time to get there. If we stay here, we can do it now. The summer arbor is a good place."

Hosteen shook his head. "Not good here. There are too many people, voices. The air vibrates with sound."

"We can send the students home."

"On the reservation, there aren't any telephone or electric wires. Your connection with your granddaughter may not be strong enough here for you to see where she is. You need to tell us more about where we can find her."

"Okay, but Han said he's not letting me go anywhere without him."

"He can come, but must stay outside of my *hogan*. I want everything to be as it was yesterday when you contacted the girl."

Han looked at Hosteen. "You just got back. Can't you wait until tomorrow? Sally just saw the prisoners while in her bed. I think you can put her in a trance in the back of the condo. She has wonderful memories of Chooli here."

"She spoke with Chooli in my *hogan*." Hosteen shrugged. "I can control her thoughts better there. Do you want to take the chance it will be better here?"

Han reached for his wife and held her for a moment before planting a kiss on her forehead. "If you go now, I can't come with you. The students need a place to meet. You made our condo a safe place for them. They read messages from families of missing girls. Some have searched for years for a lost sister or daughter. Our students talk to me about their own fears. They wonder what tomorrow will bring for them. I'll stay here and teach them some self-defense." He stepped back. "I must trust you'll be safe with Hosteen."

"Okay, we're going to Hosteen's *hogan*." Paul sprang forward to open the front door. "I'll go for Grace. We'll meet you out front."

The girl with the hand drum stopped when Paul entered the condo. Grace jumped up from her seat and ran to him. "Any news?"

He shook his head and took her hand. "We're going with Hosteen to his *hogan* again. Your mother saw Chooli in a dream. We need to help her with a trance."

"Ann's in the kitchen. I'll tell her where we're going."

"We're going back to Hosteen's *hogan*, Ann." Grace looked at the spread of sandwiches on the kitchen counter. Baskets of food were everywhere.

Ann replied, "Families of missing girls keep arriving to pray. It isn't only about Chooli anymore. Word has spread throughout the rez that we meet here to bring peace and courage to each other. They no longer have to hide in their homes because no one hears their struggle."

"People bring food for the singers. They come into the kitchen to share their stories. Some go out back to be alone when their emotions overwhelm them." Ann filled a bag with sandwiches and water. "Take this, you'll get hungry."

They regrouped at Sally's condo. At the front door, Sally paused. "Wait, I remember something in my dream. There's a woman with Chooli named Rose. She's from Arizona and someone kidnapped her a few days before Chooli. She wants her husband to know she's alive." She turned toward Chau.

"I'm on it!" His fingers were flying on the keyboard as his eyes studied the screen. "Here's something. A missing woman in Arizona from the Apache Reservation. I'll send off an email to the police department. We'll get word to her husband."

Randy raised his head from a computer screen. "I have another email from the retired couple in New York that want to help with our search. It says, 'Hello, seekers. My wife and I have followed your quest for the missing Navajo girl. We believe we can help. I've reserved a room in the Albuquerque Hotel for us and we'll arrive in your city tomorrow. I'll explain then how we can assist. My wife, Gertie, is an experienced counselor.'" Randy printed the message.

"Call him, Randy, find out what plane and tell him we'll meet them at the airport." Melinda made a note on her phone.

The front door opened to a sunny day. White clouds hung low in a blue sky. Cactus in the front yard bloomed with red and yellow flowers. A startled lizard darted across the path. A beautiful New Mexico greeted the searchers again, as they got in the car to chase monstrous men. To find innocent victims and bring them home.

CHAPTER SIX

Clothes kept trying to escape from Gertie's suitcase as she absentmindedly stuffed in more. "Do you think we can help, Walter?"

"The young man on the phone said we can. He knows we're not spring chickens. We have knowledge of how evil works. He said that." Walter packed his suitcase with five boxers, five sets of black socks, five white shirts, and three blue cotton slacks. His comb and hairbrush were in a bag with the medications he took daily. He snapped the lid shut and moved to where his wife's suitcase threatened to explode on their bed.

Gertie came back from her coat closet with a blue cotton jacket on a hanger. She looked at her overflowing bag and sat on the bed with the jacket rolled up in her hands. Tears threatened to fall. "I keep having nightmares. I see them all again. My sister, my parents, all the others. How can humans be so cruel? Why did we survive? Was it for this?"

The sleeve of her bathrobe pulled up on her arm, exposing the faded black tattoo of six numbers. Today they reminded her of all the stories.

She was five when the Germans separated her and her sister from their parents. They became part of the "twins" experiments. Her mother's scream, as she was pulled away from her children, still rang in Gertie's head. Soldiers dragged the girls away and threw them down into a pile of crying children. Gertie's survival during those black days depended on her powerful desire to live as she fought through pain and loss. Her sisters' last breath rose and fell in her own chest. Outside the gates of the prison camp, she discovered her family was gone. She was the only survivor.

~~~~~

They arrived in America with nothing. A refugee program found the teenagers a small apartment in Brooklyn near other death camp survivors. Gertie found comfort with her neighbors. She gained weight and went to school. With her thirst for knowledge and a need to return the help she had received, she soon found herself with a master's in psychology. Over the years, she listened to tormented young girls. She heard too many stories of abuse. Sometimes, she was able to help shift an ugly past into a bright future.

Walter found work in a woodworking shop. He enjoyed creating lovely pieces of furniture from discarded pieces of tree trunks that brought beauty into a home. He found he could take a broken old tree and make it into something new. Over time, his creations became popular, and he opened his own business. Customers asked for more. He found young artists who turned discarded pieces of metal or wood into something useful for the home. His showroom of unique furnishings drew in more clientele. One shop in Brooklyn grew to a franchise across the country. He hired eager young people willing to work hard to have a business of their own. Walter became a wealthy man. After he retired, they took to traveling across the United States. Native American culture a special draw.

"From what the young man said, it's happening again. Indian girls are going missing, and outside the reservations, people are ignoring it. We vowed to never forget what happened to us. Maybe now we can make a difference in New Mexico." Walter hugged his wife, his face nestled close to her hairline. He inhaled the sweet scent of her lilac shampoo.

"We can think like the devil. We know. Gertie, if we can help them bring one back, it will be worth our being there. You can show the girl how to live again. You did it."

Gertie glanced at the tattoo and pulled her sleeve down to cover the numbers. "How long do you think we'll be there? I don't know what to bring."

"We can stay as long as we want. There's nothing here that needs us." He reached into her bag and removed four blouses and three pants. "They have stores there, honey. It'll work out."

After locking the front door, Walter pulled the suitcases to the curb.

Suddenly, Gertie remembered, "Did you stop the paper?"

"Yes, dear, I took care of it."

"What about the mail? Did you tell Terry to come for the mail?"

"Yes, dear."

A taxi stopped in front of their house, and after Gertie and Walter settled in the back seat, they held hands as they began their trip to Albuquerque, New Mexico.

Once on the plane, the couple relaxed in first-class seats. Walter looked over at his bride of over 60 years. Her eyes were closed, her breathing had slowed to an even rhythm; he remembered the first time he saw her.

~~~~~

The war left Germany in shatters when it ended. Refugee camps were set up by the Red Cross across the country. In 1945, the mass liberation of the death camps created chaos everywhere. Walter walked through the camp in search of food. The moment he saw Gertie was etched in his mind forever. She was sitting on a bench alone, tears on her face. When he sat down next to her, she looked up at him. "I'm alone, the Nazi's took all of them. What am I supposed to do?"

He covered the marks on her arm with his hand. "I'm here. We'll figure it out together." He went to a Red Cross tent and came back with chicken soup and a blanket for her. They found lodging together in a tent with other survivors. Days became weeks, and two years later, they were told they could migrate to America. They married at the camp before leaving. One couple among thousands of refugees who found themselves without family. They married to find comfort with another survivor who understood their loss.

He hadn't been in the death camps. He and his older brother, David, joined the resistance. They both survived and found themselves in a refugee camp after discovering their family had disappeared. David migrated to Palestine. Walter traveled to America with the pretty girl he met sitting on the wood bench. He found her on his first day in the refugee camp and became her protector. She returned his care with a gentle touch and a lifetime of love. They learned to speak English and started their own family in America. They named their daughter Theresa in memory of Gertie's twin sister. Walter never stopped being thankful he found Gertie.

~~~~~

A sunny day greeted them at the Albuquerque airport. After collecting their luggage, they walked through the departure gate and found two young men holding up a cardboard sign that read: *Gertie and Walter Feldman.*

Walter introduced himself to the sign holders. "Hello, I'm Walter and this is my wife, Gertie. Thanks for meeting us. Is there news about the girl?"

A Navajo boy introduced himself. "Hi, I'm Randy. "The news is good and bad." We know she's alive and with three other girls in a cave. Her grandmother saw her in a trance. They have a connection. The bad news is we don't know where. It could be anywhere from Arizona to North Dakota." The boys brought them to the Albuquerque Hotel in Old Town to settle into their room and gave Walter a cell phone number to call when they were ready to meet the crew.

Walter paced the hotel room while he read from the sheaf of papers the students handed him. The numbers of missing girls were larger than he first thought. He studied when the girls disappeared, where, their age; and finally, where bodies were discovered.

Shuffling the stack of papers on the bed, he moved pages around to form several piles. Then he took a few pages from each pile to make another one. "This is it, Gertie. We need to have those computer whiz kids find cases like these. The disappearances are in the spring. The families say they are not runaways. They found girls' bodies in the same locality. Up north. We need to find patterns and get a tighter picture of the kidnappings. The monsters will use what they did in the past that worked. I'm calling the kids to come get me. Do you want to rest or come too?"

Gertie stopped unpacking. "I'm coming with you. They said the girl's mother isn't there. She went to a medicine man's cabin to call on their Navajo ancestors for help. I can see if any of the young people need support. They must be frightened. The statistics are about girls their age." She sighed and put a box of tissues in her bag.

CHAPTER SEVEN

As Paul drove by the Albuquerque Airport, Sally watched planes flying overhead. She imagined passengers returning home, staring down at the city from behind the plane's windows. Families waited inside. Others were leaving New Mexico, possibly for good. People in the plane windows were unconcerned about the blue Mustang they may have seen on the highway or the red pickup truck that followed discreetly behind.

Hosteen Begay sat in the back seat with Sally and held her hand. His head rested on his chest. The pulsing beat of his fingers danced across her palm. Images flashed behind her closed eyes. She saw herself walking down paths to hidden caves. She looked for the one with Chooli. Over and over, she peered into the darkness and listened for voices. She sneezed when dust rolled down the walkways. Colored stones stuck out from walls. Quartz sparkled in the dim light. She saw bones she described to Hosteen and heard water drops. Hosteen identified dead animals from the bones and described stalagmites and stalactites forming from the trickles of water.

An hour passed and her only insight was a sketchy history lesson from Hosteen. She opened her eyes to look out the car window. "I can't find her. I don't feel her anywhere."

Barbed wire fence stretched for miles across the prairie. Their car passed pickup trucks pulled to the side of the road with turquoise jewelry for sale on the back bed. Young Navajo women sat on folding chairs ready to show their wares to passing tourists. "Maybe I can't find her. The girls could be anywhere. This whole adventure could be for nothing. This country is enormous. It could take a lifetime to search everywhere." She frowned at the idea of defeat.

In the front seat, Grace's head bent forward. A shudder rocked her shoulders. When she turned, her eyes blazed. "What are you saying? There are many people helping us find Chooli. We have help. More come by the hour. I believe in you, Mom. You will find her. Trust Hosteen. He knows what to do."

"I'm trying, Grace. She's far away from me. I see snatches of her. If only I could get close. Time is running out. I heard one of the girls in the cave say there was a truck coming for them."

Grace's face flushed. "You promised me you would find my daughter. You said you wouldn't desert me again. Mom, you're my only hope that I'll see Chooli again. You can't quit."

Hosteen interrupted, "We're close to my *hogan*. Are you ready for what you may find this time? It could be more frightening than before. In your dream, you saw four girls. You heard words of pain. The cave may have more than girls. They may have used the cave before."

Sally nodded. "Grace seeks her child. I won't give up. I promised her I'd find Chooli."

From the front seat, Grace reached for her mother's hand. "Thank you, Mom. I'll be there with you."

Their car stopped in front of Hosteen's rustic *hogan*. Paul got out of the driver's seat to open Sally's door. As she stood next to him, his blood-shot eyes stared down at her and in a strained voice he said, "I never liked you and Chooli having secrets. You had private talks. She always wanted to be with you. I hated you sometimes for having more of a connection with my daughter than I had." His chest rose and fell as he pulled in air. A muscle in his jaw twitched. He hung his head. "I know I wasn't a good father. My drinking drove her away from me. I'm grateful for your connection. You've given us hope we can bring her home."

She looked at her desperate son-in-law. "You're a good man, Paul. You and I have a bond, too. We love the same girls. Together, we'll bring your daughter home."

Sally reached to hug Paul. His chest shuddered in her arms. Tears pooled in his dark eyes. One slid down his cheek. Sally caught it with her finger and held it in front of her. She smiled. "We'll make it happen."

Hosteen rushed past the group from the car. "I need to take care of something inside the trailer." He opened the front door and disappeared into a dark interior.

"He looked upset. I wonder what made him disappear so quick." Grace stopped next to Sally. They both stared at the shut door.

Paul joined them. "Come on, we can wait for him inside the *hogan*."

"Do you think he's okay? He moved fast," Grace asked.

As they walked to the *hogan,* a breeze blew across the mesa. Sally felt a chill and looked at the red cliffs behind the *hogan*. Paul stopped and also looked at the cliffs. "What do you feel?"

She shook her head. "Just a chill, an icy breeze. I wonder if it came from the mountain."

He looked up and followed Sally's pointing hand. "Come, we'll go inside and wait for Hosteen. We need to find the cave."

Inside the *hogan,* Sally fidgeted. Something felt wrong. An eternity later, Hosteen appeared at the door and scanned the distant mountain. He seemed to listen to the wind. A hawk flew overhead and dipped its wings in front of him. It circled above the *hogan* and flew low to the ground as it made for the mountain. Hosteen watched the bird disappear and whispered words.

~~~~~

The red truck passed the cut-off that led to Hosteen Begay's *hogan*. It stopped around a bend up the road. Two men got out and raised binoculars to their eyes. They watched people leave the car.

Cliff put his binoculars down. "I don't like the nosey old Indian getting involved. His reputation as a seer on the reservation ain't good for us. The kid keeps crying for the old lady." Cliff, a man in his early thirties, wearing an old Levi jacket and western shirt that matched hundreds of others in the area, peered at the *hogan* with bloodshot eyes.

His companion, Fred, stared at the four people leaving the car. "Maybe we should get rid of her. She's been nothin' but trouble since we nabbed her. They put posters up with her face all over Albuquerque. Someone's been posting stuff on the computer. Lots of eyes are looking for the Navajo girl. I need to make her keep quiet. Show her how her life is gonna be from now on. When we get back to the cave, I'll take my time with her." He spat a wad of yellow phlegm at the ground that barely missed his brown cowboy boots.

"You can't leave marks on her. She's valuable the way she is. Let's wait here for a while, see what those folks are going to do." Cliff pointed to the group headed toward the *hogan.*

"Look Fred, it's our job. We gotta transport the girls from the snatch to the meeting with the buyers. It's usually easier than this. No one knows they're missing, or goes looking for them until after they're with their new owners. The lucky ones get to join some Sheik's harem. That's where the kid is going. Might be some old guy's favorite for a while. As long as she stops blubbering. The other girls are goin' to bordellos in Mexico. I've been doing this for six years now. The money's good. Usually over within a couple days. Then I get to go home to the wife and kids."

Fred looked down at the *hogan.* "Wish I could keep one. Don't like livin' alone. Would be nice to have a live snatch waitin' for me at home. Tried it once with a girl I picked up in a bar. She left after two days. This one I'd keep locked up. No way to escape."

"You can't. The cartel is too big to fool with their merchandise. I want no more trouble than what we got down there. Take your money and go to Vegas. Live it up for a few days. You can buy whatever you want there." Cliff put the binoculars down. "Doesn't look like much happening. We should go back to the girls."

~~~~~

Inside the *hogan*, the bright New Mexico did not penetrate the closed door. Dim light from a side window showed colorful cushions on the floor. Sally inhaled the sweet perfume from the hanging plants. The interior of the *hogan* welcomed her. Hosteen Begay sat cross-legged on the floor. Grace spread pillows in the four directions and sat across from Sally, pounding the hand drum with a padded stick. Sally listened for her heartbeat. The air inside transformed to a scent like high mountain pine. She closed her eyes and allowed her heart and the sweet pine to carry her to Chooli.

"You saw Chooli in a cave yesterday." Hosteen spoke in a soft voice. "Today, we will look for the cave. Before you saw Chooli, where were you? Look around and tell me what you see."

Sally's eyes closed. She blocked out the *hogan*, her daughter, and son-in-law. Her mind concentrated on Chooli as she searched for the cave.

Desert sand blew across her face. Large and small cacti next to her feet. More, she needed more. She saw trees, brown earth and a truck, no, a white van. It was the van that had taken Chooli from the mall. She looked around and saw a trailer: it was small, old. The door hung open at an angle. It had been there for a while. A broken bike, a wood picnic table, empty glass bottles, and tin cans scattered on what appeared to be a front yard. Turning, she saw a dirt road in the distance. It cut through the trees. Where was the cave entrance? As she scanned the hillside behind the trailer, the skin on the back of her neck began to tickle. Her hands stung with pins and needles. A call from a hawk pierced her trance.

The screech came from outside the *hogan.* "Someone else is here Hosteen. I don't like it." Goose bumps rose on her arms. Powerful hands held her tight as she came awake.

"We must go." Hosteen helped her stand and hurried her toward the *hogan's* door. "The hawk called a warning. There is danger nearby. We can't stay here."

"But I want to see Chooli. It's too soon."

"We can't stay. The kidnappers have found us. It's not safe here." Hosteen turned to Paul. "They are dangerous people and will do anything to keep their prisoners from being found. Anything! Including getting rid of us or them. We need to warn the computer students to shut down. No telling who we're dealing with."

Sally shook her head. "We can't go back. It's more important than ever that we find Chooli fast. I won't go back with nothing. There must be someplace else."

Hosteen stopped outside the door to look at the Hesperus Mountain peak. He fingered the bear fetish around his neck. His mouth moved with silent words. A hawk swooped down in front of Hosteen. The bird's eyes studied the human in front of him before flying up and away toward the mountain.

When he turned to speak to Sally, she saw a man years younger. The lines on his face had smoothed out. "There is a Sacred Place. My father took me there as a boy. Deep in the mountain, away from people, there is an old burial ground and *kivas*. I heard voices there. The Ancients told me their stories. They told me about buffalo hunts, how they brought food and honor to their families. My father built us a shelter. We stayed for many days. I listened to the voices and learned how to use plants to heal, to speak to the animals and to be strong in the face of danger. I still go there for lessons. We'll be safe there."

Outside, Paul reached for his cell phone. "I'll call Han to say we're going further into the reservation and let him know someone followed us. Most likely from the condo. He should shut down the computer kids and send them back to school until we know more."

Grace put her arm around her mother. "I've heard of the place Hosteen will take us. Many say there is magic there."

After Hosteen gathered herbs from the *hogan's* ceiling, he ran to the door of his trailer. He returned a few minutes later to the waiting searchers, and they climbed into the car. Grace turned to her mother. "For years, I have heard stories of how Navajo elders go to the Sacred Place to speak with their ancestors. It is said that long ago Navajo tribes went there to hold ceremonies of thanksgiving. It was a place of peace and joy. Then one day the white man's army came and slaughtered the people. A few escaped and fled north, away from the white man. Since then, there haven't been ceremonies of joy. It is a lonely place. Only a few know how to find it. You will see Chooli there."

Outside the *hogan*, Paul took his cell phone from his pocket. "No bars. Can't make a call from here. He moved to their car and helped Sally and Grace inside. Hosteen reached in and gave Grace the dried plants he had cut from inside the *hogan*. "Here, hold these, we'll need the power of the plant people where we're going." He slid into the back seat next to Sally.

When the car started down the road, she asked. "I saw you talking to the hawk earlier. How do you do that? It looked to me like you sent it away. Where to?"

He reached for her hand. "You ask many questions. I can't give you simple answers. When I was a young man, I went on a vision quest. I stayed alone in the forest for four days without food. I fell asleep. When I woke, I found a hawk standing next to me. I heard it tell me it was time to go home. When I arrived home, I asked my father why the bird spoke to me. He told me the hawk choose to be my spirit animal guide. From that day I can hear and talk with hawks. I have a connection with them, like you have with your granddaughter."

"I wouldn't believe you if I didn't see it for myself." She closed her eyes and allowed her head to fall back on Hosteen's shoulder.

Paul moved the car away from the *hogan* and drove north, further from Albuquerque. "We delivered messages on the rez long before cell phones. I can get a warning to the kids in Albuquerque the old way. They may be in danger." His first stop was a trailer five miles away. The news delivered, he moved on. They headed deeper into protective shadows of the Sacred Mountains.

At the trailer, an old, bent-over rodeo rider got into a pickup truck to deliver the words. Paul's message would travel through several more stops and arrive in Albuquerque, safe from intruders.

~~~~~

Further up the hillside, the two men returned to their red truck. They didn't follow the car. Once on the highway, they headed toward Arizona.

"We got to move them," the man with the brown boots growled. "It's too dangerous to leave them where they are. Call the boss, find out where we go next." But the cell phone didn't get enough bars to make a call. The red truck occupants moved away from the mountain on reservation roads until they reached I-40 in Gallup. They turned toward Arizona to return to their prisoners.

CHAPTER EIGHT

A bump in the road jolted Sally's head from Hosteen's shoulder and onto the seatback. "Ow, what was that?" She opened her eyes to look out the side window. They were on a barren, rocky landscape in the middle of nowhere. Reservation dirt roads were sparse with amenities, such as filling in holes or removing hidden boulders, but usually there were tire tracks to follow. On this road, if it was a road, there was nothing to show other vehicles had ever been there. The sun was above them now and ahead were more rocks and tumbleweeds. The Hesperus Mountain in the distance marked the northern boundary of the rez.

Paul called, "We're here." The car came to a sudden stop. Sunlight cast a golden glow on three rocks in a row in front of the car.

"I see nothing. Are there caves here?" Sally discovered her leg muscles were stiff and nerves tense. "I thought we were going to find caves. How can there be caves here? It looks flat. Are you sure we're in the right place?"

"Hosteen brought me out here when I was trying to kick the booze habit. Demons took control of my brain. I remember struggling to breathe and fighting off monsters. Hosteen called on the ancestors to bring me strength. I owe my life to this place. There are hidden markers on the ground. Rocks and plants point the way." He pointed to a small stone perched on top on another.

Sally started to get out of the car, but struggled until Grace's hand reached in to help her. Grace's tangled black hair, creased shirt, and defeated eyes urged Sally to move. Grace must feel unbearable pain when she worries about her missing daughter.

Grace said, "this is *Diné* country, very few whites have ever been here. We're in a sacred village of the Ancestors, safe from prying eyes or ears." Grace turned around and waved her arms in an arc to encompass the rocks and dirt in front of her to show an imaginary village. "I believe they'll help you find Chooli. She talks to them when she's troubled. I believe she prays to them now."

Hosteen led them down an almost invisible trail. Soon, their car disappeared behind a wall of rocks. The ravages of time and weather had altered what had once been a two-story building made of blocks of stone. Logs held the rocks away from what looked like doorways or windows. More stones placed there by Anasazi led to an open doorway. Sally remembered a trip she went on long ago with friends to Chaco Canyon. Their guide explained the history of the Anasazi. The Navajo call them the Ancient Ones. They built villages of rock throughout the southwest thousands of years ago. Great care was taken to make *kivas*, storage rooms, burial chambers and multi-story structures. For an unknown reason, the villages were abandoned, and the Anasazi disappeared. Today's historians have reasoned it may have been a draught over several years that caused them to leave, or to escape an enemy. But where did they go? Structures that rival today's architects were left behind.

Hosteen continued to walk through the rock-strewn land. Ruins appeared as silent sentinels of the past. Time and weather had scattered fallen rocks near their feet and sunlight left shadows on an otherworldly scene. Pottery shards lay scattered on the ground. Sally stopped to pick one up to examine the pattern of white lines.

"Mother, each pattern was a signature of a clan member. The artwork on the pots told a story." Grace held up another piece of broken pottery to show Sally.

"It seems as though the people were just here. There are so many pieces. The colors are beautiful." Sally bent down to replace the pottery piece. "I'll leave it here for someone else to enjoy."

Grace replaced her piece and smiled at her mother. "You think like a Navajo."

"We cannot stay here." Hosteen moved away from the rocks. "We're going into the *kiva*." He continued to lead them, now faster, his long legs striding forward.

Muscles in Sally's legs stretched as she tried to keep up with her guide. She clambered over a boulder, careful to not cut herself on the sharp edges. When she was about to call for a halt in what had become a mad scramble, she saw it. A massive rock-lined round hole in the ground, maybe 20 feet across and 10 feet deep. She had been to the Great Kiva at

Chaco Canyon and knew the importance of the *kiva* as a sacred place for the clans to call upon their gods for help.

Hosteen stood over the hole. The tips of his boots touched the rim. Wind blew across the *kiva* and dust wrapped around his feet. "When he was a young brave, my grandfather found this place. He had been hunting and stayed here for a day and a night. The bright stars kept him awake that night, and he had a vision that he would become a great healer. He brought my father here as a youth and my father brought me. It was here that my father taught me how to speak to the 'People.' We smoked a pipe with plant leaves he took from the pouch around his neck. I watched the smoke spiral up from the bowl of the pipe. I heard my father chant next to me. The column of smoke became a cloud, and I saw the face of a man. He spoke to me. I heard his words in an ancient language I never heard before. But I understood him. He told me it was my destiny to be a healer. That I must learn how to make medicine with the plants, how to hear the voices of the lost. My family shares the gift of hearing the Ancestors. I come here for lessons. Pueblo people used the *kivas* long ago for ceremonies. We will go inside and you will see Chooli." His face softened as Sally approached the hole. "I'll help you down, there is a ladder."

A hawk screeched. Sally looked up to see a bird circling overhead. Hosteen nodded toward the hawk. "He will guide us." Hosteen disappeared behind a pile of rocks and returned with a wooden ladder. He lowered it into the *kiva* and climbed down.

"I don't know if I can use the ladder." Sally stood and peered into the hole. "It looks rickety to me."

"It held my weight. It's not too far to the bottom. I can catch you if you fall. We have work to do here. It's your turn to be brave." Hosteen took a stance below her.

Sally turned and stepped down. In no time, she stood next to Hosteen.

Grace stood at the edge and called down. "Paul said he will return to the car. He'll keep watch with binoculars for intruders. He was careful to drive here in a round-about way, and didn't see anyone follow us. Still, he wants to make sure." She then climbed down the ladder to join Hosteen and her mother.

Rocks lined the *kiva* walls to form a sturdy structure. Along the circular wall, an occasional flat stone stuck out like a shelf. Hosteen saw Sally studying the rocks.

He said, "They could have been used to hold a light for ceremonies held at night."

Drawings of spiral circles made Sally think of families. Huge flat rocks were set along the walls of the circle that could be used for benches. There were many benches to make room for a large group. Sally wondered about the people who had sat in this *kiva* before her. What did they ask for? She closed her eyes so she could hear and feel Hosteen's chant and steady drumbeat. A gentle push from a whisper of air, a flash of light, and she felt herself joined by yesteryears families.

She thought about the cave where she saw Chooli held captive. She tried to find it. A hawk called, and she looked toward the sky. She squinted her eyes to search above for the unusual cries. Suddenly, a shadow fell across the land in front of her. She looked up and the hawk's red eyes gazed down on her. It hovered above her. It called again. She felt herself become lighter and, with a gentle lift, became one with the bird. She wrapped arms and legs around warm feathers. A breeze rocked her forward, and she leaned into the wind. Hosteen's words floated away as she heard the hawk's screech.

White clouds surrounded her. Blue sky ahead. High above the earth, she saw a landscape of trees, a trailer, dirt road and human debris.

She traveled above the dirt road to a blacktopped road, then a store, and a sign read "Roger's." The building was old, with a red roof and white gas pumps in front. She saw more trees, another camper, children playing, a dog, and a horse. Where was the cave? She talked to the hawk. "We need to find the cave." The hawk rose higher above the prairie and circled. She peered below, searching for a dirt road. There! Sally shouted and pointed down to a run-down trailer and a hole in the nearby hillside. Then Hosteen's voice said, "We can go inside the cave now."

The hawk flew down and Sally felt her feet touch the earth. The entrance to the cave was in front of her. Ahead, the air smelled stale. The cave was silent. And empty. Blankets that covered the girls lay on the floor, along with discarded food wrappers.

"No one's here, they're all gone." She gasped in pain as she doubled over and sat on the ground. They were too late. Breath came in ragged gasps. Each hurt as it traveled from her lungs to her heart. She balled her fists, fingers dug into her palms. She closed her eyes and cried out, "Where are you,

Chooli?" The cry came as a plea. Her head fell forward, and she pulled her eyes open again. Then she saw lines scratched into the dirt floor next to her feet.

A long line was broken by a shorter one. It appeared to be a cross with a small stone placed on the top line above the diagonal line. Someone had left a message. But who? And what?

She felt a pull from behind. Hosteen's voice drew her away from the abandoned cave. Her opened eyes met her daughter's. "Grace, I'm sorry."

Drinking water from a canteen Grace handed her, she told the story of what she had seen. She drew a picture in the dirt of the scratched cross and placed a stone where she remembered seeing it in the cave. Hosteen studied the message and looked to the sky. He spoke words to the clouds, to the wind and the wandering tumbleweeds.

Sally looked up to see what he saw and moaned. The hawk was gone. "I felt myself become lighter and lift off the ground on the hawk's back. Through the bird's eyes, I saw the world beneath me. I found the cave and more, a store, another trailer, people. Maybe we could locate the cave with the store." She stopped to take a long look at the sky. Tears pooled in her eyes. "But she's not there anymore. We're too late."

Hosteen said, "I've sent the bird to find Chooli. She is alive. It's time to return to the computers. The scratched message shows us where to look." He murmured a prayer and tossed corn pollen into the air.

The threesome climbed out of the *kiva* and picked their way through the deserted village to return to the car. As she stepped around the crumbling rock walls, Sally thought about the people who had once called this place "home." She didn't see where there could have been water or proper soil to grow crops. Where did the enormous tree trunks come from? Only scraggly plants grew now. She reasoned food would have to be brought here.

Paul waved as they got closer to the car and called, "Did you see her?" A headshake from Sally caused him to frown. He raised a bottle to his lips to drink.

Grace glared at him and the bottle.

He handed the bottle to her. "It's water! My daughter needs me to be alert and strong. Don't worry, there's no gin here, not anymore. I lost too much time away from you and Chooli with my drinking. No more!"

Paul moved away from the car to hold his wife. "I didn't see anyone watching us. You were alone. I watched the hawk head north after it circled you. Are we going back to Albuquerque?"

Hosteen said, "Yes, we have work to do there. There is important information for us there."

~~~~~

As Paul's car took to the road, a white van in Arizona headed north. It traveled on the Interstate Highway 25 at the speed limit.

"I don't know why we're goin' to the goddam Sioux Reservation. We oughta be gettin' them girls to Mexico. I've had enough of waitin' on 'em." Fred looked out the front window. "There's a stop ahead. We can fill up the tank and get some eats. I'm hungry."

Cliff answered. "I'm not sure we should stop for long. I gave them light doses of the sleep drug. We don't need to be driving around anymore than necessary with the cargo in back."

A gray hawk flew overhead. It screeched as the van turned into a gas station.

The van pulled up to a gas pump. After filling the tank, Fred pulled over to the side of the yard. "I'll check the girls and then we can get some burgers."

~~~~~

Chooli heard the call. She closed her eyes and concentrated the way her grandfather had taught her. The gray bird flew high above her. Her grandfather had taught her to listen to the words of the wildlife. She felt the bird watching her. It came closer, and she saw the silver feathers, the piercing orange eyes. The hawk fluffed its wings and Chooli felt a warm breeze touch her. She listened for a message.

"Stay strong. They come for you. Your grandmother sees you. She hears you. Tell her what you feel, what you see, what you hear. They are close."

A hand touched her shoulder. "Grandma, is that you?"

"No Chooli, it's me." Rose whispered, "You were talking. It's best that we're quiet. The men are in front, but they stop and check on us. They're taking us to some kind of meeting place."

The back door opened and Fred peered in at the girls. They lay crumpled in a pile, not moving. He grinned and slammed the door shut. "They're all out cold, let's go."

Chooli looked at the door. A line of light shone into the back of the truck. "Look Rose, I don't think the door's shut all the way." She moved over and pushed at the door. It opened a crack, and she peeked out. She saw a table and bench in a grass area in front of her. A line of trees behind. The men were gone.

"Rose, I can open the door. There's no one out there. I'm going to get out of here. Come with me."

Rose shook her head. "I'm afraid. They said they'd kill us if we tried to escape. Stay here."

"I've got to try, Rose. My grandfather taught me to be brave." Chooli wrapped the blanket around her shoulders and lowered herself out the back. She ran from the van to the picnic table and ducked underneath. The trees were only a few feet away. Could she make a run for it? She whispered, "Grandfather, I don't know what to do."

"Where do you think you're goin', girlie?" A hand grabbed her foot and pulled.

"Help, someone help." Chooli yelled. She kicked at the intruder.

"No one here to help you." Fred yanked again and pulled her clear of the table. He held her ankle and dragged her back to the van. Still holding her by one leg, he pulled her up to the steel bed and pushed her inside. "I'll take care of you later, little one. You'll regret what you just done."

A hawk screeched. Fred looked up at the sky. "Come on, Clint, we better get going."

Rose held Chooli in her arms. "Did he hurt you? You were brave to leave. Stay brave. I saw a hawk outside when the door was open. My people believe in the bird people. I think the hawk is outside to help us. It screeched when Fred grabbed you and threw you in here. I pray your grandmother will find us in time."

~~~~~

The van slowed down and stopped. Fred got out and opened the van's back door. Rose and Chooli sat against the wall. Rose had her arms wrapped around Chooli. The two Lakota girls were next to them. Their eyes wide open.

"So, you're awake. All right then, stay quiet or you get another needle to put you to sleep. Mama Lady, move away from the little one. She'll be on her own soon." He laughed, spat a tobacco plug next to Chooli and grabbed her foot. "I gotta teach you a lesson. No one escapes from Fred." He climbed into the back and pushed at the door to close it behind him. "Can't leave any marks on you, but I can show you what you got comin' real soon. Hold still." He began to climb over Chooli, but Cliff slapped him on the shoulder and pulled him back.

"I told you to leave her alone. She's bought and paid for the way she is. Give 'em all some water and a candy bar. I wanna' get to the meetin', get rid of them, and spend some time in Vegas with our money."

The van returned to the highway. A hawk flew high above the highway. His shadow rested on the van's roof.

CHAPTER NINE

As they drove back to Albuquerque, Sally described what she had seen from the hawk's back.

Paul asked questions at staccato speed. "Was the building adobe, wood, stone? Was the sign old, rusted, what were the colors?"

"I'm not sure Paul. The hawk was high above the ground. I saw things go by at warp speed. I remember seeing a front porch, red, but it was a blur, it was so quick. The hawk seemed to search for something." Sally rubbed her forehead. "There was a car, old, dirty. Wait, I remember the license plate had Arizona colors. We must have been in Arizona." Her head fell back against the seat pad. "That's all I got. Wish it was more."

Grace held her cell phone. "Mom, I recorded everything you said so you can relax. Paul is going to stop with the questions. Isn't that right, Paul?" She reached over and gave his arm a hard squeeze.

"Okay, I'll concentrate on driving. I'm getting hungry. We're close to Gallup, how about we stop for breakfast?"

They left the reservation dirt road at Gallup and Paul pulled into a gas station to refill the tank. A restaurant next door looked like a good place for needed sustenance. When they were settled in a booth, they ordered breakfast and Sally called home.

Han answered. "Did you find Chooli?"

"We didn't find Chooli. I found the cave, but it was empty. They moved the girls. I saw some landmarks and Grace has my memory recorded on her cell phone." Sally took a deep breath and heard a whistle in her chest. She felt physically and emotionally drained.

A long minute's silence from Han before he said, "I'm sorry for you and Grace. If Chooli wasn't there, she's alive somewhere else. You'll find her and bring her back."

Sally smiled. "Han, it's wonderful to hear your voice. How are things there?" After a pause, while she nodded and pushed a button on the phone. "I'm putting you on speaker so everyone can hear. Are the students still there?"

"They left to go to their jobs. I've been thinking about you and am worried. We've had visitors. A man in a pickup truck came to the door. The man had a white beard and looked like an old cowboy. He had on a buckskin jacket, jeans and old cowboy boots. He said Hosteen had a message. They didn't have power for cell phones at his *hogan*, so the message is being relayed by the Moccasin Telegraph. The message was that everyone had to go further into the reservation to get away from people watching. And that bad people may know where our condo is, so everyone should be careful. I made him pancakes for breakfast. He said he had business in

94

Albuquerque and left a card. The card is for selling wood stoves."

"We went to a *kiva* deep in the Navajo Reservation. Is there more happening at home? I hear voices in the background," Sally said.

"A man named John is here from Arizona. He is the husband of the woman in the cave with Chooli. You said in your trance that a woman called Rose takes care of Chooli. He answered Randy's message looking for a missing woman in Arizona. His wife is Rose, and she has been missing for a week. He brought a cute little girl with him. I like him. He said he can help find caves. Come home, you need rest and other people will help."

"We're on our way. In Gallup now."

"Neighbors have a room for Hosteen. I made room here for Grace and Paul. You need to come home. The couple from New York that answered our call for help have come here too. They're staying at the Albuquerque Hotel. Gertie has helped girls who had trauma in their lives. She talked with the students and listened to their fears that they won't find Chooli in time. It's her life's mission to help. Her husband, Walter, told me how they came to America from Germany after the second World War. They will tell you their story when you get here and you'll understand why they have come so far to help. We have fierce people here. I miss you." Han's voice cracked with emotion.

"I miss you too. We'll be there soon." She closed her eyes to stop the tears before she pressed the off button.

It was no fault of the restaurant that the food tasted like cardboard. All they needed was to refuel. The travelers ate in silence. Coffee made tightly strung nerves bounce in Sally's stomach.

Back on I40, no one spoke. Hosteen held the bear carving around his neck and closed his eyes. His lips moved soundlessly. The scar above his eye turned bright red, displaying his inward stress.

They would be in Albuquerque in an hour and a half. Sally held her bear pendants in a tight fist. She played out scenes in her head of her granddaughter with her in the future. She listened to Chooli's laugh.

~~~~~

The street in front of her home was quiet. No rushing students or cars. The travelers were met inside by Han and an elderly couple.

The woman introduced herself. "Hello, I'm Gertie Feldman and this is my husband, Walter. We came here because we believe we can help. I've been talking to the teenagers, and I'd like to spend some time with you, Grace. Will you come outside and have tea with me? I want to share my past with you. The reason I'm here and why I believe I can help you." She looked to her husband. "Maybe Walter can spend some time with Paul. He's been talking to John and they have some ideas he'd like to discuss with him."

Han brought Sally into their bedroom for private time and Hosteen went next door to the prayer vigil.

In the kitchen, Gertie poured two cups of tea and put them on a tray. "Can you open the door, Grace? It's beautiful outside. We can sit under the arbor."

Grace nodded, grabbed a plate of cookies, and followed Gertie out the back door. The afternoon sun brightened the outdoor patio. Fragrant plantings brought a relaxed order to their surroundings. They settled onto an outdoor lounge chair, and Gertie placed the tea with the cookies on the table in front of them.

Grace sipped the tea. "My mother has been so strong in the search for my daughter. So much has happened. I don't know how to relax. I don't know if I ever can again."

Her hand began to tremble. A strong squeeze on her hand and she looked into Gertie's eyes. Then her shoulders shook, and she fell forward onto Gertie's shoulder.

"I should have gone with her. She was alone in the mall. If I'd been with her, they wouldn't have taken her. But my being a lawyer was more important than helping my daughter buy a prom dress. I needed to make a court appearance. I told Chooli I was sorry I couldn't go with her. She would enjoy herself with her friends. It was my place to be with my daughter." Grace balled her fists and pounded her legs. "It's my fault. What if we never find her?"

Gertie held the frightened mother. "I was the only one in my family who lived through the holocaust. I felt my twin sister's pain when she died." Gertie pulled up her sleeve to display the tattooed numbers. "I was a child when they took us for twin experiments. I blamed myself that I was hiding when they came and took my sister for the last experiment. If I had been there, maybe they would have chosen me and my sister would be alive. I remember the fear I felt back then, every day."

"You told me you know your daughter is alive. Hold on to that. You're her mother. You can feel her and she can feel you. Your love will give her needed strength."

Paul opened and closed the back door with a bang. He stood still for a moment and blinked several times. "I've been looking for you. We need to plan what to do next. There's plenty of people here. We don't have time to sit around chatting about old times."

He walked over to where Gertie and Grace sat. "Walter filled me in about your past. You can help when we get Chooli back."

Grace's face turned red. "Paul, stop it. You're being a bully. I need to talk to someone about how afraid I am that we may not find Chooli. Mom has Han to help her. I need you, but you don't hear me. Go back inside. I'll come when I'm ready."

Gertie wrapped her arms around Grace as Paul opened the back door and returned to the condo.

~~~~~

Han studied Sally's eyes. "I can give you some acupuncture to help with the headache."

"Good. Do you have something for my stomach, too? Have you heard anything more?" Sally wondered if the missing students meant bad news.

He shook his head. "No news here. The students have school work. They said more people are watching for the girls. Rose's husband said he can help with finding the cave in Arizona. He has friends everywhere. You gave an excellent description of the store and how to find the cave. John called the Arizona State Police. They are checking with all the police agencies."

"She isn't there anymore. The cave was empty in my vision."

Han held her shaking body tight. "John said maybe the kidnappers left something behind that would say where they were going. Arizona police have forensics. I'll make you tea for the stomachache."

The house phone's ring ricocheted off the walls. Grace grabbed for it before it disturbed her mother's rest. A look at the screen showed the call was from the Arizona State Police. "Hello, did you find Chooli?"

"Sorry, Ma'am, I don't have information about Chooli. This is Sergeant Baxter from the Arizona State Police. Our men were able to locate the store and trailer that Mrs. Li described. We should be able to locate the cave that the girls were held in, if this is the correct store. I'm faxing pictures to the Albuquerque police. They should bring them to you soon. I have detectives waiting to go out there. Have Mrs. Li call me back at this number 555-145-7880."

Grace took a deep breath. "I'm Chooli's mother. She's alive, we need to find her quick. Tell the detectives she's alive. Find her." Grace put the phone down, as she could no longer talk.

Ten minutes later, an Albuquerque police car with flashing red lights arrived. Two officers got out. Grace raced to the door.

The condo's living room began to fill with police: John, Paul, Walter, Grace, and Gertie. "Show these to Mrs. Li, see if it's the same place. The Arizona police are ready to go into the cave and get trace evidence. It will help to find where they're going." Excitement showed in the officer's face. "We're close."

Sally fought through a fog of fatigue to go into the living room to look at the pictures. There was the store the hawk saw. Rogers. The yard was familiar. "Yes, that's it. The trailer is the same, too. Are the police there now? Are they going inside?"

People crowded around Sally. The police pointed to objects in the photos. Everyone talked at the same time. Sally gasped for breath. "I need air, I'm sorry I can't answer any more questions." She pushed to break free. In a moment, the world went dark.

She woke in her bed. Startled at not remembering how she got there, she began to get up, but Han's hand was pressing on her shoulder. His dark eyes held hers. He said, "You stay here. You scared me when you fell in the living room. You've been rushing around everywhere. Let other people help to find Chooli. You can't do everything. I have a drink here to help you relax. Many people are at work now in Arizona to find Chooli." Han helped her sit up to drink the tea.

"I am the only person with a connection to Chooli. I have to find her." She closed her eyes and fell back.

~~~~~

Paul looked at the pictures and pointed at the picture of the trailer. "It looks like a hunting camp. Lots of those in the mountains, probably on private land. If we contact hunting clubs, we may know who the men are."

John shook his head. "It might work, but it would also tell them who we are if they belong to hunting clubs. And they probably do if they've thought this out as much as I think. They've done this before." He couldn't say the word "kidnapped." John sat with his daughter in his arms. He smiled down at her sleepy eyes. "My wife is with your missing girl. Mrs. Li said she saw Rose talking to her granddaughter. Rose is alive. But for how long?" John shook his head. "I don't want to take a chance they'll harm the women."

"There's another way." Paul pointed to one picture. "I have rodeo friends who will help. A brotherhood won from years of riding and broken bones. The scum we are dealing with are not rodeo. They have no respect." He looked at the picture again, touched the mess next to the trailer. "See, there isn't anything here that speaks 'horse.' I can get the riders to search. A posse."

"I can get bikers to look." John reached out to shake Paul's hand. "A posse."

"It's time for me to return to Arizona. I'll leave my little one with my mom, spend the night, and be back here in the morning so we can coordinate our men for a search. Paul, we got to believe our girls are alive. That we will find them."

Paul shook hands with his new friend. "Soon buddy, we can do it."

CHAPTER TEN

Coffee aroma lured Sally out of bed. Grace, Paul and Hosteen sat with plates of food in front of them at the kitchen table. Their conversation came to a halt, and faces turned toward her when she entered.

She shook her head. "Sorry, I didn't see Chooli last night. Nothing new."

Grace studied her mother. "You look better this morning. Han made us pancakes for breakfast. I don't remember when I last had pancakes." Grace pushed food around her plate. Her fork stopped at a morsel of pancake, stabbed it with fierce determination, and then dropped it into her mouth. She chewed, swallowed, and returned to concentrate on manipulating her food.

Paul sat hunched over in a chair, peering at a cell phone. Pancake crumbs on a plate in front of him. He briefly looked up when Sally said, "Good morning." Then he returned to the phone.

"My guys are looking for the red truck and white van. So far, they've found hundreds of trucks and vans, but nothing with our girls. They could be anywhere. They got to move sometime and when they do, plenty of Navajo and Apache warriors are ready to pounce on them. Damn them, I want my daughter back. Gonna call John to see if he knows something new." He punched buttons on the phone. "No answer." He put the phone into his back pocket. "Don't like feeling helpless. I'm her father. There's got to be something I can do." He stood and paced across the kitchen floor.

Hosteen moved from the table. "Come, Paul, we'll go outside and listen to the messages the morning light sends us. He opened the outside door and stepped aside for Paul to walk past him into the bright sunshine.

Han held out a cup of coffee for Sally. "Do you feel better? Are you ready to eat?

~~~~~

Hundreds of miles away, in South Dakota, Chooli looked at the breakfast bar the repulsive man tossed at her. The crumpled wrapping paper was dirty around the edges. Her stomach ached and the idea of any food made her feel sick, especially this thing. She threw it back at the man's feet.

He reached down and pulled the blanket off her. "If you want this back, eat. You're going to your new home soon, can't be sick." He held the bunched-up blanket above her head and stared into her eyes.

Chooli shivered and backed away from him. With the blanket gone, she remembered the last time he took it from her. They had been in the van for hours when they finally came to a stop. Frank opened the back door. "Good, you're all awake. Everyone out." When Chooli moved toward the door, he stopped her. "Not you, little one." His filthy hands reached for her. She shrieked and kicked at him with her bare feet. He laughed and moved closer.

The other man had come and pulled Frank away from her.

Chooli remembered the rough hands. The odor of the sweat on his body. The foul smell coming from his mouth. She reached for the blanket.

"Nope, you don't get it back that easy." He hooted and held the blanket higher.

Rose moved close to her and held the breakfast bar out. "You need to eat to keep your strength up. Drink water. You're dehydrated." She held out a bottle of water. "Please, drink and eat."

The man peered at Rose and threw the blanket to her. "Give this to her when she eats. I gotta get my food. Be back later."

"I can't. It makes me sick." Chooli shook her head. "I don't want to be a slave. That's what they said I'll be."

Rose held the bar to Chooli's mouth. "Think about your grandmother. She's looking for you. She came to you in the cave. You have a connection. Use it. Close your eyes and call to her. I think she can hear you when you reach out to her." Chooli turned her tear-stained face to Rose as she reached for the water. She sipped from the bottle and took a bite from the bar.

When will this be over? Rose began to shake. She had been a prisoner of the vile men for what felt like weeks. It had been dark in the cave, and bright sunlight from the only window in the shack they were in now had her disoriented. She didn't know what day it was or what time it was. If only the girl's grandmother would find them. She dared to hope, and she called out to John. "John, I'm here, I pray someone will come for us. Hear me." She turned to the young girl. Chooli had her eyes closed and her lips moved.

~~~~~

The coffee cup fell from Sally's hand. Hot coffee splashed her legs when the cup shattered on the tile floor. Grace pushed her chair back to grab her mother.

"Chooli!" Sally stared at the broken cup, afraid to move. Her legs trembled, and she swayed. Han's arms reached out to hold her. She looked into his eyes. "She's calling me, I hear her." Sally rambled. "She wants to come home. She's terrified. I saw her. She's sick. Wants us to come for her."

The kitchen door opened and slammed shut as Paul rushed in. "Did you see where she is? Anything to give us an idea of where to look."

Sally looked at his face. "It was fast, like a flash of light. I saw what looks like a room, not a cave."

Hosteen appeared behind Paul and took her hands. "Close your eyes. You can see more. Hold my hands and take deep breaths. Chooli reaches out for you, you can hear more. Listen."

A shudder ran through her arms at Hosteen's touch. Eyes closed, she called, "Chooli, where are you?" Then, "I see her face. She's saying something. I can't hear her. Nothing. Hosteen, I need to be in a trance now, here. She's so close. Hurry, help me, please."

"You can do it yourself. Your mind has the memory of how to find Chooli. We can go into your bedroom, where it's private, and I'll sit with you."

Sally ran to her room and sat on the bed. She breathed in the familiar odor of the sage smoke from her diffuser. Her hands twitched on her lap. Dust tickled her nose. *Chooli, where are you?* In a moment, the scene materialized in front of her. She described what she saw to Hosteen.

There's dust on a floor. Sunlight from a window. They aren't in a cave anymore. This looked like a cabin with walls and a ceiling. The only window is barred. Girls were lying on mats on a metal floor. The two girls from the Lakota Reservation are holding each other near the window. Chooli is scrunched in a corner as far away from the others as she can get. Rose is near her eating something, maybe a candy bar. Two men are sitting at a metal table playing cards. It looks like they're drinking from bottles of beer and there's an ashtray full of cigarette butts.

Hosteen's voice intruded. "Look out the window. Do you see anything?"

Could she see out the window? Slow steps through the debris on the floor, and the window was in front of her. "All

I can see outside is desert. The white van is there. Nothing else."

"Grandma? I sense you're here. I heard a man say we're in South Dakota, near a runway for planes. They're taking us to Mexico." Chooli moved to get up on her knees, but she swayed and sat back down with a thud.

Fred slammed his cards down. "Hey, over there. Be quiet, I got to concentrate here. I told you, no talking. I dunno, this might be my last trip. The plane ain't gettin' here soon enough. Can't take much more of these blubbering girls."

Cliff stubbed out a cigarette. "I doubt if they'll let you, Fred. The cartel doesn't let go. You signed up for life."

Fred walked to each girl. Gave them a nudge with his boot and returned to the table. "Okay, let's play cards."

Sally stood still, barely breathing, while the man moved around the room.

A tug from behind told her Hosteen was bringing her back from the trance. "No! I want to stay with her." She struggled as more hands pulled at her. When she opened her eyes, she was in Han's arms and Hosteen held her hands. "I want to be back in the trance where I can hold Chooli. It's the only way. Hosteen if you can hear me while I'm in a trance, then I can tell you when they move the girls. I can go with them. I saw two men in the cabin, they're talking. If I get close, I can hear, I can tell you so much more if I stay there."

Hosteen nodded. "It could work, but what if the plane gets there before us? I haven't left anyone in a trance since I worked with the twins. You're taking an enormous chance.

You might end up in Mexico, out of my reach. We could lose your spirit. I don't want it to happen again."

"We have to find a way. I heard one man say they were waiting for a plane. If I can hear more, you can send help. I need to be there. Hosteen, if I can feel when you tug at me to leave a trance, there must be a way to connect me to you so you can hold on to my spirit."

Han moved so her head rested on his chest. "I'll hold you. My heart will beat with yours. You will come back to me."

Sally drew in a breath. "I hear your heart. Do you think it will work?"

A nod from Han. "I'll keep you safe. Here, listen for my breath. We can do this together."

She looked up, "We can do this, Hosteen. When the time comes, I can be with Chooli, and Han will keep me safe in his arms."

"It could work. You have a strong trust with your husband. Maybe you can do it." Hosteen took her left hand and placed it in Han's hand. "When it's time, let the gold from your rings join you as one."

CHAPTER ELEVEN

Paul paced between the summer arbor and the kitchen door. He stopped for a moment to listen to the morning birdsong. Yet nothing helped his shattered nerves. A tantalizing odor of bacon and pancakes drifted through the open kitchen door.

When he entered the condo, the din of frenzied voices assaulted him. People at the kitchen table were chatting intensely. He found himself in the living room and returned to nervous pacing, circling around seated students. Their fingers ceased tapping on keyboards, eyes left the laptop screens and watched him. He stopped before the front window that revealed the street, stood still, and closed his eyes. He imagined a car arriving and his daughter jumping out to greet him with a joyful, "Hi Dad!"

Reality rushed in and he shook his head. Chooli was gone. The voices behind him came from many people who were helping in the search for his daughter. He needed a drink . . . just one . . . to settle his nerves.

"Grace, I got an errand to run. Be back soon." He escaped the house and ran to his truck. With a tug from his trembling hand, the truck door opened. The engine roared as he sped down the street. The neon sign out front beckoned. *Mike's Bar*. Paul pulled to a stop out front, jumped from the truck, and pulled open the door. Inside, the air reeked of cigarette butts and stale beer. Its walls were plastered with posters advertising the various beers the bar served. The only sounds came from two scruffy guys shooting pool in the back in the dim room. Paul looked in the mirror behind the bar. An old man looked back. After several minutes of a stare down with himself, he found a seat and pulled his head into his shoulders.

"What'll you have?" The short, gray-haired man sported a friendly grin.

Paul shrugged. "I dunno, gimme a shot."

"Comin up." A moment later, a shot and bottle of beer materialized in front of him.

He inhaled the delicious, all too familiar aromas. He would savor the taste as he reached for the shot glass, his hand shaking uncontrollably. His reflection in the large mirror revealed the shell of a man. A man alone, without family, with nowhere to go. He reached for the drink. The person in the mirror spoke to him. "*If you drink it, your life will end now, here in this dark, dank gin mill.*" He dropped the shot glass, spilling its contents and knocking over the beer. A puddle of beer and cheap whiskey pooled on the bar.

Paul slid from the barstool and pulled a handful of bills from his pocket. His hands shook so much he couldn't count them as he dropped them on the bar. "Here, sorry for the mess."

The bartender slid the money back to Paul. "Keep your money. Drinking ain't gonna solve any problems, buddy. I'm not interested in getting guys dead drunk here."

Out on the street, Paul stepped into his truck and sat there, his heart racing from the near slip. He had done it. He said no to the irresistible urge. Where to now? He looked into the rearview mirror and slowly turned his grimace into a grin. He needed to be in one place and turned the key. The engine roared to life.

He found Grace in the kitchen at the house and moved to her side. She glanced up at him. "I thought you had an errand. Is everything alright?"

"It got canceled. I'm here to show support to the helpers." He kissed her cheek and grabbed a couple bottles of water from the fridge. "I'll bring these to the kids."

~~~~~

Chatter in the living room continued as Paul brought in refreshments. Cell phones rang with news from the University's branch in Gallup. Students there searched the web for information on all missing native American girls. The Gallup search found reports without a follow up. Thousands of dead ends. They gathered information to report to the media. A pile of pictures of missing girls throughout the southwest, north to the Dakotas and Alaska, grew on desks. Someone needed to be accountable. Each time the students found an old missing person report, a name was added to a list on a wall inside the school. The search for Chooli had morphed into a national search.

Randy scrolled through message boards on his laptop screen. "It's been quiet for eight hours. I don't like that. People may be afraid of being tracked. Too many of our girls have disappeared. We need to take action. Let the world know."

"Wait!" Chou jumped up. "I've got something. A report from South Dakota, near Pierre. Lights seen in the prairie. The report is vague, almost like they're afraid to say anything." Chau read from the screen. "At our camp in Kadoka yesterday. I saw a light outside. Far away, fifteen to thirty miles. Hard to judge how far. There's an old camp used by travelers. Dark now, I don't know what happened."

Chau hunched over his laptop, his fingers flying over the keyboard. "I'll see if I can get a better location. I got a map of the area up on my screen." His search began with a prayer of finding a thread of information to follow. He read the names of towns from the map in front of him. "Murdo, Kennebec, Kadoka. There're miles of open space in between."

Sally sat with Han on the living-room sofa, half aware of the student's voices. She had been resting her head on Han's shoulder, but lifted it to face him. "I heard that name, Murdo. I heard someone say that."

Conversations in the room stopped. All heads turned toward Sally.

"Do you remember more? Who did the talking? Any sounds?" Chau peppered her with questions.

She closed her eyes and took a deep breath. Silence. She shook her head. "Nothing. I was in a trance. I remember

Chooli and Rose talking. I tried hard to hear what they said. There was a lot of noise, girls were crying, and someone banged on the floor with a chair." She opened her eyes. "I'm sorry."

Hosteen came into the room. He glanced at the computer screens as he passed by the students and stopped in front of Sally. "You remember more now. You heard the name of a place in South Dakota. We can go somewhere private and listen for more messages from Chooli and the other girls. I can help you remember more of what you heard. Where can we go to be quiet?"

"My garden. I've a bench there. I grow some plants from my home back east and I go there to relax. But will we remember what I say if we're alone?" Sally moved from Han's embrace and stood.

"I'll come with you." Han stood next to her, took her hand and looked at Hosteen. "She's been through too much stress. She doesn't eat. I'll stay with her."

Hosteen shook his head. "That's not a good idea. You might distract from what she hears. She hears your heart and breath when you're close. I won't put her into a trance. She has the memory of what she saw and heard. I can help her remember more." He walked with Sally through the kitchen to the back door.

~~~~~

Sally sat on the bench with Hosteen and bent her head up to feel a breeze cross her face. She ran her fingers through her hair. A tumbleweed wandered down the hill in back of her garden. She inhaled the sweet aroma from the garden flowers. This was her special place. She'd put in local plants, and some flowers from her home on Cape Cod that she'd researched would grow in the southwest if raised with care. In a few moments, stress lines left her face. She was ready.

Hosteen talked to her in a slow rhythmic voice. "What do you remember about the room? Not what you heard. What did you see?"

She closed her eyes and searched her memory. "I saw the girls, Chooli, Rose and the two others. They were dirty, crying. Rose had bruises. There were water bottles on the floor, food wrappers. There was a toilet and a sink. Chairs. Everything looked old, chipped, broken, filthy." She opened her eyes and looked at Hosteen. "Nothing there to say where they are."

He reached for her hand and held it in a firm clasp. "Now tell me what you remember hearing. What did Rose say to Chooli?"

Sally closed her eyes, but this time, she wrapped her arms around her chest. She sought Rose in the room. And then she remembered seeing Rose kneeling next to Chooli. "I remember, Rose said she heard the men talk about being in South Dakota." Her eyes flew open, and she jerked forward, startled that she'd remembered the words.

"Good. Did you hear the men talking? Maybe they were behind you, you didn't see them, but you can hear them. Breathe deep, block out what you heard from Chooli."

"Okay."

"Now, what did you hear?"

"I heard mumbling behind me. I remember someone said they were waiting for the contact. Two men's voices. One said they had a high-priced load this time. A deep voice, he sounds old. The other is younger. I think he's the one with the brown boots. He said the pretty kid was worth more, since she's a virgin."

Sally opened her eyes. "They're talking about Chooli!"

"Try to remember more of what they said." Sally watched Hosteen's hand reach for the spirit animal on a leather cord around his neck. "Hold the bears you wear. They'll bring more strength."

She closed her eyes again and clasped the silver and turquoise bears hanging from the cord around her neck. "I remember they said something about an airfield. The plane was due after dark. I remember the words Murdo Airport." She slumped over in Hosteen's arms. "They're taking them tonight!"

Hosteen stood and pulled Sally up. "Come on, we need to let the kids know of this fresh development. We need to get to South Dakota."

Han pushed the kitchen door open and rushed to Sally. He took her from Hosteen's arms. "Enough. She can't do more."

"Yes, I can, Han, I have to. I heard the men say they're leaving tonight. We have to find her. Otherwise, she may be too far away for any hope of a rescue."

Sally entered her front room, which had recently morphed into the *war room,* and waved to get everyone's attention. "I remember a conversation in the cabin where Chooli is being held. It's near Dakota, South Dakota. A plane is on the way tonight to take the girls away. We need to go there. Can anyone of you figure out transportation, or how?" She stood in front of the students, a new strength forming her stance. She was ready to do battle.

Chau looked up. "It's 970 miles from Albuquerque to Pierre, South Dakota, the closest airport to Dakota. About fourteen hours' driving time. The best way for us to get there would be by plane. Does anyone here have a contact with private pilots?"

Hosteen walked over to Chau. "I do. Some pilots at the Albuquerque Airport have done private flights for me in the past. I'll make a call. Someone needs to alert the police in Pierre that a plane is coming to pick up kidnapped girls."

The room became silent as Hosteen used his cell phone to make a call. He spoke into the phone in Navajo and, after a few minutes, nodded his head, smiled, and held the phone out in front of him. "We have a ride, just need to wait a couple of minutes to get instructions. Who's going?"

Grace ran into the front room from the kitchen. "Chooli's in South Dakota? How do you know that? I missed out on how you found her in South Dakota. I need to know what's happening. I'm her mother. If you're going after her in a plane, I'm coming."

"I remembered hearing someone talk about being near Pierre. Grace, everything moved quickly." Sally looked at Hosteen. "I'm coming. Grace and Paul and you. Who else?"

Han squeezed her hand. "I'm not letting you go alone. I'm coming. What about John? When he left to bring his little girl back to Arizona, he said he'd come back here. I've his cell phone number. I'll call to find out where he is. He'll want to come with us. His wife is with Chooli."

After the number appeared on Han's contact list, he sent a text message. "I got him, he's just outside Albuquerque, he'll be here in a few. He's coming."

The computer kids began to chatter again. Voices had a new sound, success in their venture was near.

Hosteen's cell phone buzzed. He looked at the screen. "This is it. A Citation is getting ready for us. It'll get us to Pierre in less than two hours. The pilot needs to file his flight plan, do his routine inspection, and we're off. We need to be at the airport in an hour. Is everyone ready?"

Tears filled Sally's eyes. "Ready!"

Ten minutes later, John's powerful motorcycle pulled to a stop in front of the condo. He jumped off and ran inside. "I broke all records on getting here, sure was lucky no cops on this trip. Any word on when we're leaving?"

Hosteen answered, "I'll call for a ride to the airport. I wanted to wait for you. Our plane leaves in half an hour."

John turned anxious eyes to Hosteen. "How much does the plane cost?"

Hosteen smiled, "There are charter planes with Navajo pilots that fly without charge for emergencies. Relax, you'll be with Rose soon. But you better give the key to your machine outside to one of the college kids here. It should be somewhere safer than the front of the condo."

John scanned the students and pointed outside. "Does anyone know how to ride my bike? It'll need a rubdown with a cloth as soon as it cools off."

Randy jumped up. "I'll take care of it for you. I'll bring it around back. It'll be safe there. She's a beauty. I've a bike, but nothing like yours." Eyes shining, Randy grasped the key and ran out to admire the two-wheel wonder.

~~~~~

A six-seater van came and took them to the area for private planes at the Albuquerque Airport. A tall young man in a brown leather jacket met them. "Hello, I'm Dennis Yahtzee, and I'll be flying you to Pierre. Follow me and we'll get started." He turned to leave, but spun around when he recognized the medicine man. "Hosteen! It's good to see you again, old man. Are we going on another rescue mission?"

He turned to face the rest of the group. "The plane I'll be operating belongs to a well-known celebrity. I'm not at liberty to give his name. All I can say is he supports our efforts to rescue girls from the cartel. I'll bring you to Pierre and wait for you, then bring you back here. Come and check it out. This is a really comfortable aircraft."

On the most luxurious plane she had ever seen, Sally strapped herself into the padded recliner seat. "This is wonderful." She settled in for the less than two-hour ride to the Pierre airport.

The plane took off at 3:00 p.m. and landed in the Pierre airport at 4:40 p.m.

The group disembarked and assembled in the nearby waiting room. Everyone was talking. Hosteen raised his voice. "We've got to get ready for what lies ahead. The Sioux police are searching the canyon where the light was seen last night. They'll send word when they find the cabin. We'll have to divide into a couple of groups to get in the police cars. I want Sally with me."

Han spoke up. "I go where my wife goes." He followed Hosteen and Sally to a waiting police car.

An officer from a second car moved toward Grace and Paul. "Come on, I can bring you and the big guy in the back in my vehicle." He motioned toward John.

John shook his head, "You guys go with the police. I got my own wheels waiting." He gestured toward a trio of black-leather clad motorcycle riders. "I'm more comfortable on a bike."

The vehicles left the airport at 5:00 p.m.

At 5:10 p.m, police officers entered a trailer in a remote canyon. They found empty water bottles, food wrappers, broken furniture, and spent drug needles scattered on the floor. But no occupants.

A young South Dakota State Police officer carefully walked around the room, searching for some sign of who had been there. "Look," he called and pointed to the dust in a far corner. Someone had scrawled *Chooli*.

CHAPTER TWELVE

"We got out of there just in time." Frank put his binoculars on the seat beside him and looked at the four semi-conscious girls sitting on the van's steel floor. Greasy burger wrappers lay scattered around their lethargic bodies. "I see lights up the road. Cars are coming. They'll be at the old camp soon." The obese man turned in his seat and leered at the girls. "My advice for you girls is to do what you're told. What you had here ain't nothin' compared to what's gonna happen in Mexico. You'll be in bordellos down there." He pointed to a girl curled in a ball, long dark hair concealing her face. "You're pretty. You might get lucky. End up with someone who'll keep you for hisself."

He tucked a dirty cotton shirt into his worn jeans, gave his sagging belly a pat, and belched. It was hot in the van. He reached across the console for a bottle of cola. A line of hamburger fat slid down his hand to his elbow. "Best burgers have lots of juice." He swiped his arm up and down on his pants' leg. "I'm gonna go in the back to visit with the Lakota girl one more time."

"Frank, you gotta stop fooling with the girls while they're drugged," Cliff said. "Who knows what they remember? Besides, the boss said to leave them alone and stay out of their sight as much as possible." The fingers of his right hand curled into a fist. Cliff moved closer to his colleague. "Stay away from them. You can have all you want in Mexico when we get rid of these." He pointed with his thumb at the girls.

"Yeah, but it's hard to resist. Helpless, that's the best way. You're getting old, Cliff." Frank lurched toward a girl trying to stand.

A screech from outside brought the conversation in the van to an end.

"What's that?" Frank looked out the van's front window. "A hawk! Damn bird is flying in circles overhead. Gimme the gun, Cliff."

"No, we can't shoot it. We're not that far away from the old trailer. The folks down there might hear. Besides, the bird's probably after a carcass of some big cat's kill."

Frank moved away from the window. "I don't like this. Look, it's flying lower and lower. He looked right at me through the window. I swear the eyes were red as fire and its beak was big enough to take my arm off. Look, I got goosebumps. I never saw one of those birds so close." He put his arm up to protect his face and pushed back on the front seat.

"He can't get in here." Cliff got up. "Come on, we'll go to the back of the van with the girls. We can wait back there until the plane comes."

Frank stood, but continued to watch for the bird through the van's front window. "The plane ain't gonna get here fast enough." A scraping sound near his feet caused him to look down. "The girls are moving. They're awake." He watched the youngest girl curl up and whisper. "Grandma!"

~~~~~

John and his motorcycle friends left their bikes behind the cars in front of the cabin and walked forward. An officer raised his hands to hold them back. "Sorry, you can't go any further, we're looking for car tracks out here and you can't get inside until an all clear is sounded."

John leaned over to look behind the officer. "My wife may be in there. I need to go in."

"You can't go inside. All I can tell you is the cabin was empty when we got here. We're looking for any information left behind that may tell us where they are now."

The car holding Sally, Han and Hosteen was stationed near an outdoor firepit. Sally gazed at the ashes. "Where are you now, Chooli?" Suddenly, her nerves jumped, and she jerked her head up. "I hear Chooli."

Hosteen turned and reached to hold her hand. "When the men moved the girls from here, it's possible they're taking them to the rendezvous with the plane. We need to find the girls. Chooli's calling for you. Use your connection to go to her. You remembered hearing someone say Murdo airstrip, while you were in a trance. They may be there. I'll call the hawks for help. They're near and will help stop the kidnappers." Hosteen called to the police. "We need to get to the Murdo airstrip. That's where they are. A plane is coming for them. There's no time to lose."

"Get in the cars. We're ready to leave." The police ushered the Albuquerque people into their vehicles. Red lights flashed as cars sped onto the road.

The motorcycle riders called to John. "Come on, get back on the bike. We know a way to Murdo cross-country. We'll get to the airstrip before the cars."

John ran to the nearest motorcycle and settled himself behind his new friend. The experienced rider called back to him. "Hang on, it's going to get rough." He and his friends sped into the desert.

~~~~~

Sally sat in back of the police car with Han. She said to Hosteen sitting in the front. "Hosteen, I've got to go to Chooli. I have to reach her." Leaning forward from the back seat, she grabbed his shoulder. "Help me. Please."

He grabbed her hand. "Hold on to your bear fetishes. Close your eyes and see yourself with Chooli. Believe that you can be with her."

She reached for the bears, then stopped and slipped the gold wedding ring from her finger. "Han, I need to go to Chooli. This time it may be different. I'm going to hold on to her. I can't let them take her away. Hold my ring. You have a powerful force stronger than any evil. I trust you can bring me out of a trance and back to you."

Han nodded. "Go to Chooli."

She closed her eyes and gripped the bears. The car bounced over a boulder in the road and was air-born for a moment. She rocked forward. When the wheels hit the road again, she felt a push from behind. She reached forward with her arms and felt something soft. As soon as she opened her eyes, she saw the girls and heard their cries.

She found herself on a metal floor, inside a van. Her granddaughter was in front of her with her arms wrapped around her legs. Eyes tightly shut. Other girls lay on the van's floor. They wore cotton shirts that barely covered their bodies. None of them moved, their eyes open but unfocused.

Sally called to Hosteen. "The girls are in a van. I think they're drugged. We have to get help for them. Somehow!"

As she reached to hold Chooli, she remembered Hosteen telling her that if she touched the girl; he might not be able to bring her out of the trance. She was in this place as a spirit. She could hear and see, but if she held Chooli, she might enter the child's world and not be able to return. If the kidnap was successful, she might find herself in Mexico. But the time to rescue the girls had come. Police cars were drawing close. The horror would be over soon.

Sally watched her granddaughter moan as if in a bad dream and pull herself into a tight ball. "Chooli, I'm here with you, I'll hold you until the rescuers come." Sally curled her body around Chooli and wrapped her tight in her arms. "I'm here now, Chooli, they're coming for you."

Chooli moved closer and mumbled in her sleep, "Grandma."

Sally whispered, "There are people looking for us. There's a hawk outside to protect us." She looked out the front window at the darkening sky. "They'll be here soon." As she gazed at the blue sky, a white cloud appeared. More clouds moved across the sky, blocking out the sun, perfect concealment for an incoming plane. Sally shuddered at the realization that the rescue party might be too late.

~~~~~

Frank watched the girls rubbing their eyes. "Somethin' feels different. I felt a breeze and heard somethin'."

"Don't get Indian superstitious on me now. Nothing here but us and them." Cliff cocked his thumb toward the van's floor.

A flash of light in the sky brought the men back to the front window. "It's the plane, he's coming. Get 'em up. Time for the transfer." Frank opened the van door and stepped out to search the sky.

A screech froze him from moving further. His hand held onto the open door. Black wings attached to an agitated hawk landed on the door frame. A head with piercing red eyes and a threatening open beak reached for Frank's arm.

"Hey! The damn bird's attacking me." He dove back into the van and pulled the door shut with a bang. Back inside, he mumbled, "There's more, an entire flock or somethin'."

Cliff peered out the window. "Hawks don't have flocks. I told you somethin' weird is going on. It's the Navajo, she keeps talking to herself." He moved around the girls, pushing at them and pulling them to stand. When he bent to pull at Chooli, he lost his balance and fell. "Somethin' pushed me!"

Frank laughed. "Ain't nothing there but air. Come on, get them out!"

~~~~~

Sally pushed at a tower of boxes against one wall of the van. Nothing happened. She was there in spirit form. She couldn't move the boxes. Putting her lips next to Chooli's ear, she whispered, "Wake up Chooli, you need to move the boxes, block the men from coming here. Chooli, wake up now, push the boxes."

The girl blinked. She got up on her knees and pushed at a pile of boxes next to her. They tumbled down, and Chooli called out, "Move the boxes. We need to block the men."

Rose called, "Is your grandmother with you, Chooli?"

Chooli pushed another box in front of the men. "Help is coming. Come on, let's fight."

Rose ran into Frank's protruding belly. He fell backward, but sat up and used his right arm as a club to smack Rose hard across her shoulder. She fell into a heap.

Frank yelled, "The next one who moves gets a smack from me! You're going. I don't care what condition you're in. The plane's here. We're all leaving now."

129

A plane glided down, its engines silent. As soon as the tires from the Golden Eagle touched the earth, the plane stopped, and the pilot lowered a set of stairs. He jumped out, ran to the waiting van, and opened the door. "Come on, we got to get the cargo inside quick. Someone's coming. I saw headlights in the distance." He stepped inside the van and pulled at one of the Sioux girls. "Come on, cutie, you got a new home waiting for you." The other Sioux girl clung to her friend, and they stumbled out of the van. The pilot grabbed both girls by their arms and herded them toward the stairs.

Frank looked down at Rose. "Well, you got yourself hurt. Got to get out of here, anyway. Come on." He grabbed at Rose's hair and yanked her up. She stumbled forward. One arm hung limp by her side. Her other arm wrapped around her waist. Bent over, she walked with her abductor to the waiting plane.

Chooli scurried backwards to the rear of the van. She pulled herself into a tight ball. Closed her eyes and covered her ears. The floor of the van shook as heavy footsteps closed in on her hideout. Cliff kicked boxes aside and stood over her. "It's your turn kid, come on now, don't be difficult. You don't want broken bones or bruises showing for your new owner." He pulled at her arm. Chooli went limp. With a jerk, he yanked her to her feet. Then pulled her out of the van to the waiting plane.

Sally willed herself to follow Chooli on to the plane. She sat in a seat with the girls. The Sioux girls held hands. Their eyes focused on the sky through the open passage. Tears and long hair covered their faces. Rose let out a scream of pain as her arm bumped an empty seat. Chooli whimpered, "It's too late, grandmother, we're leaving."

Frank sat in the seat next to Rose. "I'll keep you company. Shut up or I'll give you another swat or two."

Cliff moved up front to sit in the co-pilot's seat. Distant pinpricks of light grew as headlights advanced. The motor roared. The plane taxied forward and began to lift off.

Out of the sky, black wings hurtled toward the flying machine. Black bodies hit the engines and windshield. The air filled with shrill screams as the swarming birds vented their anger on the flying machine. Under the onslaught, the plane nosedived into the earth. Feathers fell from the sky and covered battered steel wings.

The plane groaned as metal bent. Shattered glass fell from the cockpit window. A shard the size of an open hand pierced the pilot's eye socket. Blood ran along the cheek onto his neck, ending in a sticky pool on his flight jacket's collar. His scream cut into the night.

The skinny man next to the pilot attempted to lift his arms to prevent a hawk's talons from latching into his throat. Unable to move in his seat, a gurgle of blood erupted from his throat before his head fell to the side. The hawk screamed its challenge before staring into dead eyes.

Sally screamed. "Push the door open girls, go. Run! Everyone, leave the plane. Help is near."

Only Chooli could hear her, and she crawled toward the door and pushed it open. She stood at the door's threshold, unable to go further. "I can't go."

The other girls tried to move but stopped when the rotund body of Frank stepped in front of them.

Sally screamed, "Hosteen, I can't get them out!"

Then she saw a motorcycle alongside the plane. A man jumped off and reached for Chooli standing at the open door. He pulled her off and set her on the ground. Two more girls approached the open door, and he reached up to catch them as they jumped into his arms. He yelled into the night, "Run, girls!" He pulled himself up and onto the plane.

Frank blocked his way. The rescuer's face was scarlet as he used his body to ram the kidnapper a powerful blow. The abductor fell to the plane's floor.

The victor stood over his enemy, poised to deliver a kick to the man's head. But he heard a whimper from inside and saw a woman curled up in a tight ball.

Sally held the woman and looked up into the man's raging eyes. "Look Rose, your husband is here for you." She released her hold so John could pick up his wife and carry her off the plane and to safety.

CHAPTER THIRTEEN

The girls stumbled from the plane, arms stretched out in front of them, screaming for help. Cars pulled to a stop, and police ran to the girls, holding them back from disappearing into the night. John brought up the rear with his wife in his arms.

Shards of glass and twisted metal covered the grass runway. An eerie cry came from inside the plane as metal bent and broke apart. A man's voice called for help. Sparks lit up the sky around the broken aircraft. A wave of acrid odor filled the air.

Still in the plane, Sally stood at the open doorway. Headlights approached. The first car stopped in front of the running girls, and Hosteen emerged, calling, "Sally, wake up. It's over. The girls are safe. Get out of there." People were leaving the cars. It all seemed to happen in a fog.

"I can't. There's still a man in here. He knows where the leaders are." She watched Grace run from the car toward Chooli.

133

Sally felt her body lift away from the open-door frame. She struggled to stay and scanned the damage behind her. Frank was still on the plane, alive. She didn't want to leave him there. He might get away. He was a monster; he hurt the girls and needed to pay.

Hosteen's voice called to her. *"Chooli is with Grace. They need you. Come back to me."*

Dark bodies of fallen hawks covered the ground. A few struggled to fly, their cries shrill. Was it true, were the girls safe? Confused, she held on to the doorway. "Grace, we saved Chooli. She's here." The people in front of her were real. She struggled to take the leap from the plane. Too tired to move further, she dropped her head to her chest and sat down in the open doorway.

Sally heard a voice. "Come, take one more step, you've come so far, you can't quit now, one more." It seemed like an eternity before she had the energy to push off the plane. A moment later, she was next to Han. He whispered in her ear, "It's over, we have Chooli. We found them all." His arms held her. She was no longer on the plane. Han had kept his promise. While her spirit had traveled to Chooli's rescue, he had stayed in the car and held her flesh and bones. He had kept her safe.

"Where's everyone?" She squirmed in Han's arms. He pointed toward a line of cars. She staggered forward. Chooli was there, wrapped in her mother's arms. They sat on the ground next to a police car. Grace held her daughter to her chest. A blanket covered their shoulders. Both chests rose and fell as shared breaths filled lungs, their bodies melting into each other to become one shared union.

Chooli looked small and helpless, her lips blue. "I'm freezing inside, can't get warm. Are we really safe? Where are we? I don't remember how I got here." Leaving her mother's embrace, she struggled to stand. "Where are the others? I need to find Rose." She swayed and took a step forward.

Grace stood. Her hands reached toward Chooli. "Everyone is safe. Rose is with her husband."

Sally asked, "Where's Paul? The other girls, are they okay?" Her breath came in short blasts. "The birds! They saved us."

"All the girls are safe. Paul and Hosteen are with the hawks. They're saying prayers to give the birds safe passage to their next life." Han loosened his grasp to allow room for him to face her. "I never want to be that frightened for you again." His dark eyes held hers for a moment, and then he placed a tender kiss on her forehead.

"Han, I need to be with Hosteen and say goodbye to the hawks, too." She stood on unsteady legs to go toward the wreckage. "Where did the police go? I see their cars. I don't see them."

"They're here. Officers from the Rosebud Reservation have taken Frank from the wreckage. People from the reservation will clear away what remains of the plane and bury the bodies of the pilot and co-pilot. Tonight's nightmare will disappear." Han took her hand. "I'll bring you to Hosteen and the hawks."

Hosteen wasn't alone. Men from the reservation searched the wreckage and gathered what remained of the hawks' bodies. They placed broken wings on blankets spread on the ground. Birds became whole again as the men painstakingly found smashed bodies and replaced exquisite feathers. Hosteen whispered a prayer and placed a turquoise stone with each bird.

Paul stood to the side and held a bird wrapped in a blanket. The hawk was alive and struggling, one wing hung loose by its side. Its open beak and red eyes held a menacing glare. Sally walked toward it and touched its head. The hawk immediately lowered its head, pulled in the left wing, and settled down into the blanket. "I flew with you to find Chooli, I remember. You brought the others to stop the plane. Thank you." The bird's eyes locked with hers.

"This one will live." Paul said and handed the bundle to her. "He's yours. Your time together created a bond. Bring him home now."

Two men with long gray hair bound behind their heads knelt on the ground next to Hosteen. Intense eyes moved across the broken feathers and talons before them. Their voices rose in prayer as they worked as a brotherhood to honor the girl's rescuers.

Hosteen said, "I'll stay to join the Sioux Nation in sending the hawks on to their next life with the dignity they deserve." He offered her a piece of turquoise. "Take this stone with you and keep it close to the bird in your arms. The turquoise is sacred. It will help heal him. Go home with the others."

Paul brought more blankets to the men on the ground. He knelt to have words with Hosteen. Then stood and took Sally's hand. His eyes sparkled. He smiled for the first time since Chooli had disappeared. "You did it, you brought her back to us." He looked out at the caravan of cars. "You must go now. The light from this crash can be seen for miles off the reservation. People will arrive with questions."

Han pulled Sally away from the gruesome scene. "He's right, we must leave before more people come. What happened here can't be explained. We need to take Chooli away. All the girls need protection from questions now."

"The others? Rose is hurt. There are two more girls. They need help too." Sally's eyes swept over the growing melee of people.

A woman with a red scarf tied around her neck approached Sally. "The girls are Sioux. Their families have been looking for them. We'll care for them. We're grateful for your help in bringing them back to us. We'll not forget what you did here today." Her face shone with pride.

The two Sioux girls were wrapped in blankets. Each held her head low, her face covered with long, dark hair. They sat on the ground apart from the plane. Adults held their hands, announcing their thankfulness to have a lost child returned. The girls whispered pleas, asking for forgiveness.

A girl with a red scar across her cheek raised her eyes to look at Sally. "You saved me from them, but I have nothing. I'm nobody!" Angry bruises covered her legs. Blood stained her arms as she moved her hand to cover the needle scars. "I've been gone for more than a year, I think." She shook her head. "I don't know what day it is, or year. I stopped caring a long time ago. The men were all the same, they didn't care who I was. Just so long as I lay on my back for them. I have a boy. He was a baby when I got in a car for a ride to town. I wonder if he'll remember me. There were times I wanted to die. But I wanted the drugs more."

Sally reached out but was stopped by a woman holding the girl. "Yvonne has seen what we cannot imagine. She's been given drugs. I'm her clan sister. I'll care for her."

"I have a friend who can help." Sally bent to look into the girl's eyes. "Gertie lived through the holocaust. She, too, has seen more than any human should."

A nod from the protective woman. "We will bring the girls home to the reservation and someday you will return to the Rosebud to see the girls. For now, they will be nurtured in the circle of their families. They will be made strong again."

The other girl clutched a blanket tight to her body. Her fingers were white with tension. She pleaded with the man sitting next to her. "Father, I can't go home. I've been with them for months. I need the drugs. I'm not the same. Your daughter is no more." She showed him the needle marks on her arms, then slumped against his shoulder. Tears ran across his hand as he held her to him.

"Girl, you're home. Your mother prayed for your return every day. I searched the rez for you and looked at the bodies of girls found on the prairie. I believed you were alive and would return to us. Let me bring you home. We will celebrate your return." He wrapped an arm around her and stood.

Han called, "We need to return to the airport, Sally. The pilot of the Citation needs to return to Albuquerque. And it's time for us to leave this place of misery and go home." He found his wife in a circle of Sioux women. Their faces covered with worry lines. Each pressed a photo of a girl into Sally's hands.

"I don't know what to do, Han. These women have missing girls. Word of our rescue has reached the reservation, and they came here to find me. They want me to help find their missing family members. Each woman has lost a girl: a daughter, a sister, even mothers." She opened her hand to show Han photographs. "They brought me these photos." Tears filled Sally's eyes as she pulled herself away from the women. "I told them I had a connection with my granddaughter. I can't help them."

Hosteen approached the group of women. He spoke to them in a loud voice. "I'm staying here after Sally and her family leave. I'll talk to each of you and maybe we can find a strong connection we can use to locate your missing girls." He waved to Sally to leave.

She circled around the growing mass of people and returned to the reservation police car with Grace and Chooli, Han right beside her. "Where's Paul? We can't leave without him."

"I'm here!" Paul stumbled toward them. His stiff knee from the bronco fall made running more of a hop and lope. "The Sioux have taken the birds for a ceremonial burial. Hosteen's staying with them. We can go."

"Rose and John, where are they? Sally heard her voice cracking with tension.

"They're in the police car next to us. Rose is injured. A woman from the reservation made a sling for her arm." Grace appeared next to Sally. Her voice showed that she had regained her take-charge strength. "John wants to bring her home to Arizona. She keeps asking for their little girl. She needs to go to a hospital for a check-up when they get away from here."

~~~~~

Stars lit up the dark sky as cars returned to the Pierre Airport. The reservation police slid out of the front seats and opened the rear doors of their vehicles. They spoke softly to wake their weary passengers. "We're at the airport. Your plane is ready for your return to Albuquerque."

Chooli struggled when she saw the car had pulled up to a plane at the airport.

"No! I can't get on the plane."

Rose twisted in her husband's arms and screamed.

Everyone froze. The pilot said, "I got to get this plane back to Albuquerque. What do you want me to do?"

Sally stood on the tarmac. "Go. You have been more than kind to bring us here. I'm sorry your wait was so long and for nothing. I won't ever forget your gift. We'll figure something out here."

The pilot hesitated. "Look, there're plenty of people who don't like flying. There's a bus company that makes private long-distance hauls." He pulled out his wallet and dug around in it, finally producing a worn white card. "Here, phone his guy, he probably won't be happy to get a call this late, but tell him I said you need help right away." He returned to digging in his wallet and found another card. "This one has my private cell number if Jake gets testy. You keep this card in case you guys ever need a pilot again." He turned and jogged toward his waiting plane.

Grace reached for the cards in Sally's hand. "Let me call. I can explain our needs better. It's a Navajo name on the card." She dug in her bag and found her cell phone. "It's still charged and we have bars. Worth the money I spent on this new model." She walked away from the girls and punched in numbers.

Ten minutes later, she returned and raised her arm and fist. "A bus will be here soon. The driver will bring us to Albuquerque and Arizona. Get ready for a long trip. It's well over seven hours, but we should make good time at night."

Twenty more minutes and a sleek silver bus arrived. Its lights flashed as it approached the weary group. A young Sioux woman sat in the driver's seat. She wore a red shirt open at the neck, revealing silver hoop earrings and several turquoise necklaces. A single eagle feather in her hair.

"Hi, I'm Winona. It's my honor to drive this bus for you. The girl, Yvonne, that you rescued, is my niece. She's been missing for two years. My sister searched the rez constantly for her daughter. I'll bring us to Arizona and New Mexico.

There is soda and ham and cheese sandwiches in the red cooler, some chocolate donuts too. A bathroom is in the back. Relax. We're driving straight through on interstate highways. My co-driver, David, will take turns at the wheel with me. Everyone is safe now."

Inside the luxury bus, seats had been opened to make flat surfaces for people to lie down.

As she stepped inside the bus, Sally looked out the front window. She wondered about the word "safe." There were still murderers out there.

Ginger ale soothed the anxious waves in Sally's stomach and the chocolate from the donuts relaxed an incoming headache. She saw Chooli cradled in Grace's arms. Rose rested her head on her husband's legs.

Sally snuggled next to Han with her head on his shoulder. His hand rested on her arm and she closed her eyes. So much had happened. Hours ran into days. When was the last time she slept? She listened to Han's steady breath and relaxed.

A dream started with the fluttering of wings. Sally saw a fence made of rolls of barbed wire. Inside there was a hill of trash, broken bottles, filthy mattresses, battered tables and chairs, the stuff of lost dreams. A single cloud moved across the dark sky. Its shadow fell across the emptiness below. Then a clap of thunder and rain fell. The water came in large drops as if they were tears from the heavens. Sally reached up to catch the rain, to stop it from falling. No more! She watched as water pooled in her hands and turned red. Blood spilled over and fell. On the ground, bodies of girls lay in mud, abandoned. Her own tears fell as she listened to the cry of the hawks circling the girls. She watched as the vigilant birds attacked a stray wolf approach the human dump. In death, the girls and women received the protection from evil they did not have while alive. The wolf left the bodies untouched.

The black and white scene changed as Sally looked past the dump and saw green trees growing at the edge. Red dresses hung from branches. Saplings were planted inside the barbed wire. A pattern in the landscape could be seen from above, HOPE.

CHAPTER FOURTEEN

Light inside the bus dimmed as they traveled past city streets. Winona turned off the interior lights when she steered the bus onto the highway. Soft engine sounds and rolling wheels lulled the passengers to sleep.

David and the hawk occupied the seat behind the driver. He had been working on repairing an old Ford truck the night before, but volunteered to work with Winona as they often drove together and had a plan on how to share the driving. He liked being with her and secretly hoped one day she would notice him as more than a co-driver.

As soon as the bus rolled onto the open highway, the ride became smooth and the bird stirred in his nest. David placed half a sandwich in the nest and watched as the bird gulped a bite. Their eyes met, and the bird raised an injured wing.

"Hey, you're not going to bite the hand that just fed you, are you?" He slowly raised his right hand and caressed the bird's head, then ran his hand down its back. He gently folded the wing back against the body. The hawk was still staring at him, so he continued to talk. "Sally is sitting behind us. If you need her, she's there. But she's exhausted. Is it okay with you if I take over her guardian job for the duration of our trip?"

Behind David, Sally sat next to the side window and watched the landscape as the bus rolled along the highway pavement. Mile after mile, there was little change. Barbed wire fences lined the side of the road. Plastic bags, empty food containers, and other debris littered the ground. An occasional horse in the distance brought western beauty back into the picture. She looked down at her lap to see the fingers of her hand entwined with Han's. The bus rolled over a bump and she heard a soft snore. She looked into the face of her sleeping husband. She whispered. "Good. You sleep Han. The days have been traumatic for all of us. We have Chooli back. But is it really over?" She released the seat back so she could recline.

Chooli lay on the bus seat across from Sally with her head resting on her mother's lap. Sleep had finally come for the girl, but she continued to whimper as if fighting nightmare demons.

Paul sat in the back of bus sending messages on a cell phone. His lips moved and head bobbed. With a rare grin on his face, he raised his head and called forward. "Good news, guys. Hosteen says the remains of the birds have been buried with Lakota tradition. Frank has been taken away by the FBI, charged with interstate trafficking. Hosteen's getting a ride home. He says he's needed there."

The hawk turned in its nest and screeched. On the seat behind Choolie, Rose woke from her sleep, sat up, and screamed. John caught her flailing hands in his. "It's the hawk. He helped us find you. You're safe now. I've got you."

As peace descended again, the passengers heard his words, and sleepy voices mumbled quietly.

~~~~~

A blast of light filled the bus as the sun appeared in the east, announcing a new day. The hawk squawked a complaint that roused sleeping neighbors. Rose moaned as she moved to a sitting position. She wrapped an arm around her chest. "It hurts. I think I have broken ribs." She hung her head and sobbed. "The time in the cave . . . the man, Frank, took me repeatedly. I remember he said he was showing me what my future was. He did terrible things to me." She shivered. "How can I be a wife and mother now?"

John ran his hand through his wife's hair and turned her head so he could see into her eyes. He flinched as he took in her bruised face, black eyes, and a cut stained with dried blood on her chin. "Rose, I'm sorry for what you've been through. It's over now, we're going home. I love you, honey."

Rose shook her head. "It will never be over."

Their driver, Winona, broke the silence that followed with an announcement. "There's a restaurant ahead. Is anyone hungry? We're in North Platte, Nebraska, on Interstate 80. This is a good place to stop for breakfast."

Chooli sat up and curled into her mother's arms. "I can't go in there. I can't be around people. No!"

"How about if I get takeout? We can eat on the bus." Winona took the next exit and stopped near the restaurant. She looked at the hollow-eyed faces of her passengers. "I'll get coffee and breakfast sandwiches."

Sally looked out the window at a parking lot full of cars and trucks. People were coming and going from the vehicles. "Leave the bus in the back, away from the foot traffic. Our girls need privacy."

After maneuvering the bus into a spot at the very rear of the lot, Winona left the interior lights on and went into the restaurant. She returned with coffee and orange juice, along with breakfast sandwiches of egg, bacon and cheese, and two bowls of oatmeal. She said, "I thought maybe the girls had enough sandwiches."

A jingle on Sally's cell phone showed a text message. After reading it, she dropped the phone and turned a white face to Han. "It's Chau. He said for us to not go home, and John too, and to call him on a new cell phone."

"What's happening?" John's voice reached a higher decimal. "I can't take any more of this. I'll call him." He pulled out his phone.

Paul jumped from his seat and took two long strides to John. He reached over and grabbed the phone. "Wait until we have a safe phone. Chau is a smart kid. Something's happened back there. We could make it worse by using our phones." He looked at Winona. "Let's see if they have burner phones inside the rest stop. I've seen them in roadside restaurants."

Sally watched Paul and Winona walk away. "He's going to call Chau from the restaurant, isn't he?" she asked Han.

Han nodded. "If it's bad news, best not upset the girls and Grace and John."

Minutes passed. "I need to use the restaurant bathroom. I'll be back." Sally scrambled off the bus and hurried inside. Paul was talking on a cell phone in a rear booth. She slid in across from him. "Is it Chau? What happened? Let me talk to him."

Paul handed her the phone. "Hello. Chau, what's wrong?"

He answered, "There's been a fire at your condo. They must have known where you live since the beginning of our search. Maybe John too. They could have gotten Rose's home location from her cell when they took her."

Breath left her chest as if someone had punched her. Holding the phone in a shaking hand, she asked, "Is everyone alright? Was anyone hurt?" She held her breath, waiting for Chau's answer. She had known from the beginning of the search the teenagers were in danger. Neighbors and friends had helped in Chooli's rescue. Were they all in danger?

"No one was hurt," Chau said. "Someone threw a fire-bomb into your summer trellis in back of the condo. A neighbor saw the flames and called the fire department. But by the time they could get to the flames, the fire had reached the back of your home and destroyed the kitchen and both bedrooms. It was a planned move on the arsonists' part to come in from the back prairie that made it difficult for the fire department to get to the fire. We don't know how much information they have on John and Rose. Where they live. It's best all of you lie low until we learn more."

Sally clenched the phone with stiff fingers and shook her head. "No. I can't put you in danger. No more. Go home, stay safe!"

Chau said, "We took a vote and we outnumber you. We're staying on this. We plan to set up our laptops at coffee shops around Albuquerque and keep moving around. The scum are angry now. Maybe they'll make a mistake and we can locate the leaders. Give me the number of your new phone. I'll be in touch as soon as I know more."

After she sent the new number, Sally shut off the phone.

Paul reached across the table to retrieve the phone. "I know a place we can all go to and be safe." He walked away from the table while pushing buttons on the cell phone.

As soon as he left the table, Winona came up and bent over the table. "We better get back to the bus. The others will be worried."

"What can we tell Chooli and Rose? They don't need to know about this." Sally pulled in a deep breath to expand her lungs. She wanted to protect everyone. She had been in "find-and-rescue" mode. Now her adrenalin had peaked, and she was ready to protect everyone around her.

"Tell the truth, the girls are strong." Winona pointed toward the restaurant door. "We better go back to the bus and make a new plan. They may have a line on the bus too." She looked over at Paul's receding back. "Come on, we need to get going."

They left the restaurant and were walking across the parking lot when Paul caught up with them. "Hey, when I talked with Chau, he said we should probably get off the bus.

It's too easy to track with a GPS. But there's nothing to worry about. I've taken care of transportation. Two cars will be here in half an hour. One will bring John and Rose to a clinic in town." He turned to Sally. "The other will take you, Han, Grace and Chooli to a hunting cabin on the rez. John and Rose can join you there after she's had medical attention. You'll be safe at the cabin."

"What about you?" Sally asked.

He nodded. "I've something to do. You go ahead." He turned and walked away.

"Wait! Where're you going? What am I supposed to tell Grace?"

"Tell, Grace and Chooli I have business to take care of. I'll meet up with you later." He turned again before she could ask more questions.

After hearing the news, John shook his head. "I want the car to bring us back to Arizona. Rose wants to see our daughter. I'll take care of us. I'll get her medical help there."

Han studied the man. "You may be able to protect her, but be careful. We don't know how large this group is. They may know where you live."

Chooli moved to sit next to Rose. "Will I see you again?" she asked.

"Yes, always. We'll ride our horses together like we talked about. Go with your family. My husband's right, I want to hold my daughter. She needs me." Rose turned to John. "I need to be with him, too."

The time passed quickly as the bus passengers ate in silence and then used packets of hand cleaners passed out by Winona.

Winona left the bus to stand outside the door and used a cell phone to call her boss. When she returned inside, she pulled David over. "We're going to stay here until the cars arrive to take these guys away, then return to Pierre. The girls can stay on the bus where they're comfortable. We'll take another route back and use rez roads. It'll be easier to track if anyone's behind us. I'm getting a serious tingle in my gut. A warning. Something bad is going to happen."

She looked across the parking lot full of cars and trucks. "I watched behind, but it's hard to keep track of who's following on a highway. There could be trouble in any of the vehicles here. I've learned to trust my gut."

David said, "I'll take over driving for a while. You keep track if we're being followed. It's going to be a long trip back. I'll go back into the restaurant for food for us."

Half an hour later, a six-passenger Range Rover and a Toyota Cavalier pulled into the parking lot and parked next to the bus. A young man with long black hair down his back and bandana rolled and wrapped around his forehead got out of the Toyota. He stood by the driver's door and faced Winona. "Hello, my name's Storm. Are John and Rose here? I'm supposed to bring them to a medical clinic in town to have Rose looked at. After, I'll bring them to their home in Arizona."

"They're inside. I'll get them. Are you aware there may be some danger in bringing them to Arizona?" Winona asked.

"Yeah, so I hear. There was quite a mess in Murdo. I got no problem going to Arizona, got some friends there to visit. We'll be okay."

Winona entered the bus and a few minutes later, John carried a sleeping Rose out of the bus and approached the car. He looked at the Chevy and its driver. "Thanks man, I really appreciate this. My wife dozes on and off. We don't want to go to a clinic here. She wants to go back to our three-year-old daughter. I'll take her to a clinic when we're back there. How long do you think it'll be before we're home? I don't have any idea where we are."

Storm answered, "It's a four or five-hour trip from here. You get in the back with your wife and relax. I'll have you home in no time. Here, let me help you get situated." He opened the back door for John.

The driver of the Range Rover identified himself as Daniel. "I'm here to take the rest of the passengers to a safe place on the Navajo reservation. Let's get them in the Rover so you and David can go home."

Winona had been standing in front of the bus and returned to the interior to bring out Sally, Han, Grace and Chooli. David brought the hawk in his nest and placed him in the backseat. "I'll miss you fella. You'll get well and fly again."

Sally climbed in next to the bird with Han next to her. Chooli flopped down on the seat in front of her grandmother. She called to her mother. "Come on, Mom, there's room back here for all of us." Grace stopped at the door. "Where's Paul? We can't leave without him."

Daniel said, "He's joining us later. He's okay, you don't need to worry about him. Let's get you guys to our camp so you can decide where to go from there." He made sure everyone was inside, closed the door, waved goodbye to Winona, and got in the driver's seat.

He started the engine and was about to pull onto the highway, when he turned in his seat and called to Han. "Hey man, would you mind coming up front to keep me company?"

Han turned to Sally. "I think there's more than one reason why he wants me up front. You stay with the hawk. I'll see what Daniel wants."

Once in the front passenger seat next to the driver, he asked, "What do you really want me here for?"

"Keep an eye out behind for a vehicle following us. I just got a warning from Winona there may be trouble ahead."

CHAPTER FIFTEEN

The Range Rover traveled Interstate 80 for an hour. Daniel pulled into rest stops twice and allowed traffic to pass before returning to the road. At the turnoff for Interstate 25, he held back for half an hour before continuing. He reassured his passengers they were safe. Forest trees snugged up close to the car when they turned onto a reservation road. Confident no one was behind them, Daniel continued down dirt roads through Colorado for ten miles.

They passed an occasional trailer nestled under trees alongside the road and then saw nothing for fifteen minutes until a small cabin appeared on the right. A two-foot-long oblong wood sign bore the name **Stay Strong** in faded black letters. Daniel pulled in behind the cabin and came to a stop.

A man wearing a camouflage jacket, hat, and pants emerged carrying a shotgun. "Hello, folks. Welcome to Stay Strong. I turned on the heat and electric in a camper for you. Go, make yourselves comfortable. Nothing to worry about here." He pointed to a camper with a light on at the far end of a group of similar campers.

The campers edged a green field in back of the wood cabin. An oak tree stood at a distance from the cabin, its branches spread protectively over benches. Picnic tables and a fire pit were nearby. Flowers bloomed in a garden by the cabin. Birds sang while splashing in a birdbath. Tall trees enveloped the secret oasis on all sides.

Grace got out of the car and said to the camouflage man, "I think this is the place Paul goes on his hunting retreats. I would never have guessed how beautiful it is back here. You can't tell from the road."

He nodded. "Yes, ma'am, we have meetings here."

"Meetings? I thought he came here to hunt and drink," Grace said. "He didn't come with us."

"My name's Arthur Langdon." He extended his hand to Grace. "We meet here to talk about what we can do to help our people. We make plans to build *hogans*, fix cars and, sometimes, to protect women from abuse. They stay in our campers until we can find them safe homes. Paul called for help. He'll be here soon. We need to safeguard you from the kidnappers. Go rest now. I'll make barbeque later."

Chooli got out of the car and walked to the tree in the clearing. She knelt under its branches and chanted a Navajo prayer of thanksgiving. As she sang, a breeze blew across the clearing and leaves rustled. A squirrel scampered down the tree, stopped to sit up and watch Chooli for a minute, then ran back up the tree to sit on a branch and chatter down at the girl.

Grace took tentative steps to her daughter, then swayed and crumbled into a tight ball and sobbed. Slowly, her tears receded. She sat up and cried out into the sky. "I couldn't believe my daughter was taken. She's so young, so gentle, why her? The evil men who took her, they took my heart too."

She stood and reached toward the sky. "I prayed for help to find Chooli. Mom was searching for her, but I feared we would be too late. I feared I would never see my child again." Her voice shook with anger. "The despicable men didn't care . . . my child . . . so many hours, days, I spent in fear, helpless to care for my child." She turned to look at the campers. "I don't know what they did to her. How they hurt her. She's not an innocent anymore. I don't know how to help her." Out of breath, Grace once again sat on the ground. She dropped her head and cried. "What do we do now? How do we start over?"

The sun began its descent behind the trees. Sally pulled away from Han and stepped toward her daughter. "Grace, I'm here." But before she reached Grace, Han grabbed her arms from behind and pulled her back to him. He spoke into her ear. "Leave them be. They have emotions to deal with that aren't yours. You don't know what the past days have been like for them. Allow them this time for their grief."

A call came from Chooli. "Mom, I'm here. I'm okay." She stood and moved next to her mother and sat down. Grace reached to draw her daughter into her arms. Their heads touched. Eyes closed, they whispered to each other.

Sally struggled in Han's arms. "I can help." She stopped to look at her daughter and granddaughter. Each of them struggled with pains unknown to her. "They need Gertie. Do you think Gertie and Walter will stay in New Mexico for a while?"

Han answered, "Walter told me they came for this. They know pain and loss. He said it was very difficult for Gertie to survive and wonder why she did, and not her twin sister. You have a brave Navajo family. Grace and Chooli will be happy again."

Her gaze moved from her family to search the compound. "Where's Paul? Go find out about Paul. That man, Arthur, seems to know where he is. Grace needs to know."

She watched her husband go toward the cabin. Then she walked into the clearing and sat down next to her daughter. She wrapped her arm around Grace and was rewarded when she felt Grace's arm hold her.

Han went into the camper and gathered pillows and blankets. He put them on the ground beside the women who arranged themselves on the blankets, Chooli in the middle with her mother's and grandmother's arms wrapped around her. Eyes closed; they murmured words of happiness at being reunited.

Satisfied the women were comfortable, Han went to find Arthur. The door to the cabin was ajar, and when he knocked a few times, he was greeted by their driver, Daniel. Through the open doorway, he saw electronic equipment on the back wall. Lights blinked; paper fell out of a printer. A man with his back to Han stood facing a map on the side wall. He swiveled to face Han and took a fast step forward, his arm outstretched. A scar ran down his face from his left eye to his chin, with another on the right side, from mouth to ear. His left eye was white and sightless. Han stepped toward the stranger and in a moment the startled man was on this back in front of Han.

"Hey, I'm a friend. What the hell did you just do?"

David rushed forward to stand in front of Han. "Take it easy, man."

Han looked down at the man in front of him. "Sorry, you rushed at me. I just reacted. We're taught Tai Chi Chuan for self-defense in school in China. My nerves have been jumping the past days." He reached a hand down to the big man on the floor to help him up. "I'm Han Li. Friends?"

The man stood. "Look, call me Kiie. My name's Ashkii, but it doesn't translate easy in English. Me and Arthur are here most of the time. We keep this place safe. I lost my wife three years ago. Police found her car with the doors open in back of a supermarket. Haven't seen or heard from her. I was in a bar, drinking, the cops had to drag me out to identify the car. I don't know if she finally got the nerve to leave me for a better life, and is happy and healthy somewhere. Or something else." His gaze bored into Han. "Hard not knowing." He shook his head. "It's different for Arthur. Police found his wife murdered on the side of the road a year ago. He had services for her. We made this place our new home. A peaceful refuge. Away from the public, yet we're ready for trouble if it comes." Arthur's grandfather started this camp for family retreats years ago. It's been here for decades and neighbors don't take notice of who's here anymore. We keep things pretty quiet here, but are ready for trouble."

"Yeah, it looks like you're no stranger to trouble." Han reached a hand up to his own face to indicate the scars on Kiie's face.

The big man chuckled. "These? Bar fighting is usually done with broken bottles. I finally got smart after losing my eye. Been a while. Not sure what I do here is much safer."

Han held the man's steady gaze. "I think it's a good thing you're on our side."

Arthur left the screen he was watching. "Now that you guys are acquainted, we need to discuss what'd happening here. We gotta keep a look-out for the enemy. They're gonna be furious at the loss. A plane, four girls and a man alive in the hands of Indians wanting revenge. That man will talk."

"Then what?" Han stepped up to look at the wall of computers.

Arthur said, "If it were easy to catch and stop the scum, someone would have done it. The enemy has an army. A battle won isn't the end the fight. There's hardship on both sides."

He walked to the map on the wall. "The octopus has many tentacles. We can only cut off a few. Revenge has a price, but some of us think it's worth it. Each time we can make the public more aware of our missing women and girls, we stand the chance of protecting one more from being taken." He pivoted toward Han.

A yellow light flashed on the printer and a sheet of paper fell out. Han asked, "Do you know where Paul is? My wife sent me on a mission for information."

"Paul went for reinforcements. Should be here soon," Kiie answered. He looked Han up and down. "Might be a fight here later, you up for that? There's a back way out of here. A path behind your camper leads over the hill to a road that'll take you back to the highway. There's a camouflaged Jeep under the trees. Easy to find when you know it's there. You can go, bring the girls out now before anything starts."

"I can defend myself and so can my wife. She enjoys planting big men like you at her feet. I'm sure she wouldn't run now. Too much history with those guys." He pointed a finger at the screen. "David said he was taking us to a safe place. What's all the electronics for? Are you expecting a fight?"

"Good question, Han. We've had some confrontations here in the past. Not expecting a fight, just taking care. Most important is that the women feel safe," Kiie answered.

Arthur came into the cabin and looked at a screen. "Someone's on the road. A gray pickup with a camper cover." He turned to the men in the room. "Look familiar to anyone?"

All eyes stared at the screen. They shook their heads. "Best we slow them down." Arthur walked over to the electronic wall and pressed a button. Han watched a screen as a tree toppled and fell onto the road.

Daniel followed Arthur into the cabin. "How'd they know to come here? No one followed the car, I'm sure."

Han looked at the screen, at the tree in the road blocking the truck, at the computers, the lights flickering. "Chooli. They followed her. She has an electronic connection with her."

"Damn, he's right! They microchipped the girls." Arthur looked at Han. "Do you think we can check her out now?"

Han shook his head. "She's resting with her mother and my wife. I don't want to disturb them. They know where she is now, anyway. There'll be time before we move again." His stance in front of the door left no opportunity for a discussion. "But we need to notify John. He's headed for his home in Arizona with his wife. She needs medical attention. A brave Apache warrior, she got caught up in their fight for freedom, and probably broke an arm, maybe ribs too. He needs to know about the microchip. I have his cell phone number. We all have burner phones. I'll call him now." Han left the cabin to make his call.

"What do you mean, Rose has a microchip? Where?" John's voice screamed into the phone.

"We're in a camp in the woods. We weren't followed here. Our driver is sure of that. It must be that Chooli has a microchip on her. She probably doesn't know. They could have put the chips in the girls when they were drugged. I gotta go to the girls, John, it looks like there's going to be a fight here." He ended the call and put the cell in his back pocket.

The men in the cabin watched Han walk toward the girls. "That's one tough guy," Kiie remarked as he looked at Han's back. "Makes a believer out of me that our people came from China."

Arthur turned to the men in the cabin. "There'll be more men than what we see. The camper shell on the back of the truck can hold people. There's three of us and the tough

162

Chinaman." He walked to the back bedroom and unlocked a cabinet. Rifles, shotguns, and handguns were mounted inside. Each man came and took his weapon of choice.

Han knelt by this wife and touched her shoulder. Her eyes opened. "Han, is something wrong?"

He nodded. "We'll have company soon. You need to move inside the camper. Bring Grace." Sally knelt to wake Chooli, but he whispered, "I'll carry her, don't disturb her." When all three were safely inside a small camper, he turned to leave. A whisper from Sally stopped him. "I love you." He moved back to her and stroked her blond curls. "I love you too." Then he turned, glanced over his shoulder at Grace and Choolie, and dashed out the door.

CHAPTER SIXTEEN

Armed with military grade weapons and wearing camouflage, Kiie and David made for the cabin door. Kiie said, "I'm gonna go find out what the Chinaman has decided. Hope he's planning to take the girls and leave. If not, I'll stick around their camper. My gun reaches further than his arms or feet can. Do you plan on staying around here, Arthur?"

A rifle cradled in his arms, Arthur stood in front the computer screen, legs spread. "Yeah, the screens show the truck has come to a stop at the downed tree. But I don't see any movement. I'll stay here and wait to see what they do next. Are they going to leave the truck or turn around? I'll catch up with you guys outside."

Empty campers became defensive positions as Kiie and David circled the grounds, leaving behind extra rifles they could use to defend the premises if necessary.

Kiie found Han perched on the front step of the camper that held his wife and her family. "Come with me, I'll show you the path to the other side of the woods." They walked behind the camper and Kiie pointed behind a brush screen to the trail.

"There's still time for you to take your women and go. You can use the hidden Jeep.

"Sally won't run away from trouble," Han answered. "Chooli still has the tracking chip, and Grace is too weak to run. I'll stay here with them."

The two men stood in front of the trailer when Arthur approached. "No time for arguing. The scum left their truck behind and are walking toward us. They're heavily armed. Looks like ten of them."

"We have three and you with your Tai Chi . . . if you can get that close. Still wanna stay?" Kiie stared hard into Han's eyes.

Sally appeared at the open door with her arms crossed. "Three . . . and two with Tai Chi Chuan. We're staying. I trained in China for this possibility. My granddaughter deserves better than to run away a loser. You're putting your lives on the line for us. I'm here to fight."

"Okay. If you're gonna stay, you gotta get out of the trailer. If you stay inside, you're a trapped target."

"I can't move Grace and Chooli from inside. Grace has a fierce hold on her daughter. If there's going to be bloodshed, I don't want Chooli to see it. I'll stay by the door. No one's getting past me." Sally assumed a resolute stance.

Han moved on the other side of the door from his wife. "We got it covered here."

"Okay, you guys. Stay safe." Arthur left and melted into the surrounding woods with Kiie.

Voices in the campsite went silent while the moon illuminated an empty clearing. An owl hooted from a nearby tree. From deeper in the forest, another owl answered the call. Branches creaked in the wind, and rustling leaves spoke a language understood only by woodland beings. Forest animals scurried across trails, looking for dinner.

The creatures stopped chattering. An ominous quiet fell across the clearing. Han hunched down next to the steps to the trailer. Sally whispered from the other side. "The animals went quiet. Someone's coming."

A red fireball careened across the sky and fell on the first camper in the circle. The blast shook the earth. Flames filled the air with the stench of burning metal, plastic, and wood.

A second firebomb crashed into the cabin where the electronic equipment was stored. Sparks erupted as equipment died. Computer screens flashed black and white images before they exploded into pieces of pulverized memories. Empty gun cabinets disintegrated into rubble on the cabin's floor.

Both structures continued to burn when a harsh voice shouted, "We can blast all your campers before the fire department gets here. Send out the girl. NOW!"

A call from across the circle. "NEVER!"

A rifle shot hit the Stay Strong sign. It swayed from one rope and appeared to wave at the men running beneath it.

Ten intruders appeared in front of the camp wearing militia uniforms of red vests and black pants. They moved toward the campers in eerie precision, holding rifles at the ready in a show of strength. A man in the middle called out,

"We want the kid back. Send her out and she'll leave alive. Your other women too. Surrender them now and they'll continue to live in sunny Mexico. We're going to leave this camp in ashes."

From her position kneeling on the ground next to the trailer door, Sally watched the attackers move forward. The line of men split in half. One half moved to the far side of the camp. Five men on each side continued to move forward, circling a trailer before throwing in a firebomb. The camp transformed from a peaceful getaway to a violent battlefield. As the men came closer, Sally took a defensive stance. She held her arms in front of her chest and bounced on her feet, then whispered, "Just give me a chance to get close enough. Let me take down one before it's over. I'm ready."

The whispered words had just left her mouth when a bush behind her exploded. Paul emerged from behind the trailer with a rifle in his hands. "It's not time to give up. We've more men than the mercenaries. They're not getting my daughter." From behind the brush surrounding the camp, eight armed Navajo men popped out from the surrounding forest, multiplying the number of defenders.

Sally leaned back against the trailer. "Paul, thank God you're here. Chooli and Grace are inside." Her eyes on Paul, she missed seeing a red-vested attacker approach behind her.

Paul shouted, "Behind you."

She turned to see a rifle in the hands of an enemy soldier pointed toward Han. A quick spin and she sprang at the intruder. Giving him a hard kick behind his knee. "No, not my man!" The enemy howled in pain and fell, clutching his leg.

Sally tore the rifle from his hands. "Don't move." As she stood over him, another attacker rushed to take aim at Han.

The scene moved in slow motion as Sally watched, helpless to stop what happened next. A gunshot pierced the air. Han fell. Paul ran to stand over Han, raised his rifle, and fired at the attacker. His rifle clicked, silent.

The red vested man called, "Missed, now it's my turn." A shot rang out and Paul lay on the ground, blood pouring from his shirt.

Sally screamed.

Kiie was beside her in an instant. His shot propelled the enemy backward.

Gunshots sounded from all directions. Navajo men were everywhere. Their faces painted with red streaks, they rushed forward to dole out justice. Two joined David on the far side of circle of campers, facing four mercenaries. Another three came behind Paul. A large man wearing camouflage bellowed, "We're not taking prisoners. Leave now."

The barrage of gunshots ceased, and the intruders fell back, picking up their wounded as they retreated.

As soon as the gunfire stopped, Sally rushed to Han. She knelt and used both her hands to press down on his blood-stained shirt. "Han, stay strong, don't leave me. It's over, they're leaving."

He opened his mouth. Words came with broken breaths. "Take them home. You go."

"I'll take them, Buddy," Kiie said. "A medic will be here in a minute. Hold on." Kiie grasped Han's hand. "You're some tough guy."

Lying beside Han, Paul opened his eyes. "Take the girls and go. Don't want Chooli to see this."

Sally choked, "I can't leave you and Han. You're hurt." A Navajo soldier with *Yas* embroidered on his shirt joined her on the ground. He gently pulled her hands off Han's chest. "You saved him today. I'll care for him. He's right, you need to go."

"I can't go, I can't let him die." Sally sat back on her heels and watched the man next to her apply a bandage to Han's chest and move to Paul.

"He'll live, I promise. I've trained for this. Both these guys are going to the hospital. You need to do what they asked. Go."

Kiie grabbed her arm. "He's right. We gotta get out of here." He turned to look at the surrounding bodies. "I'll get Chooli, you help Grace . . . and get the hawk. We'll go over the trail to the Jeep on the other side. Hurry! We don't want you and the girl involved with the police or their questions. Yas is a trained medic; he'll care for your men. Our guys will get them to a hospital. Time for us to move."

Tears in her eyes, Sally gasped as she looked down at Han and touched his face. He struggled to open his eyes.

Kiie opened the door to the camper and found Chooli huddled under a table. She looked up at the intruder and screamed. Grace called, "You can't have my daughter!"

Their cries startled Sally as she bent to embrace Han. She pulled back and turned toward the camper. "Chooli, he's a friend." She began to stand, but heard Han gasp and dropped back on the ground next to her husband. "It's over Han, the mercenaries are leaving. You're going to a hospital. We'll be home soon." She grasped his hand and held it to her face until she heard another cry from her granddaughter. She turned her head toward the trailer door and pulled herself away from her husband.

Yas handed her a cloth. "Here, wipe your hands and go to your family. Kiie can look pretty scary. You need to help him get your family out of here."

Standing at the trailer door, Sally called, "Chooli, this is Kiie . . . a friend." She stepped into the trailer and stood next to the man with scars on his face. "Let him carry you. He won't harm you. We must go now. Close your eyes, don't look at what's outside." She turned to peer under the table at her granddaughter. "Come on, I'll explain everything."

Grace reached for Chooli and pulled her out from under the table. They both stood on wobbly legs in front of Kiie.

"We need to move fast. Let me carry you." He reached down to pick up Chooli. "Close your eyes. You don't need to see what's outside." He pressed her face toward his chest and made for the door.

Grace took a tentative step to follow her daughter. "Where are we going?"

"There isn't time to explain, Grace. We need to go. I'll be with you as soon as I get the hawk."

Sally reached for the silent hawk nestled on the bed in the back of the camper. Cradled in her arm, she lowered her face to feel the silken feathers and breathe in the wild animal scent. "We must leave here and I'm leaving my husband behind. I need your strength, my friend." She felt its calm breath on her face, wrapped her arm around the nest, and moved next to Grace.

As they stepped out the door, Grace screamed, "Paul. You're hurt." She stood frozen in the camper doorway.

Sally pulled her daughter close. "He's alive. There are medics here to help. They'll bring him to a hospital. Your husband saved us. He brought reinforcements to the fight. We have to go." She released her daughter and grabbed her hand to pull her away. With the hawk's nest in her left arm, she wrapped her right arm around Grace's waist to help her walk. They navigated down the camper steps, around the bleeding bodies of their husbands, and followed Kiie to the path through the forest to a dirt road with parked cars and trucks.

Navajo men in camouflage knelt by two wounded comrades. Their conversations stopped when Kiie entered with Chooli in his arms. A man with a bandage on his arm called to Kiie. "Hey man, is that the girl? Are you Chooli?" Kiie answered, "Yes, Carl. This is Chooli and her mother."

Carl moved to stand next to Chooli. "It's good to see you. You're safe now." He rubbed the bandage on his arm and brought his hand to cover his face. His shoulders shook as he moaned.

Kiie placed Chooli's feet on the ground. He turned to Sally and said, "We found his daughter dead alongside a dirt road a year ago. He volunteers every time we ask for help in rescuing girls."

"Did all these men come to rescue me?" Chooli asked.

Kiie nodded. "Your father brought them here in case there was an attack by the men who captured you." He turned to face Grace. "Paul put out a call for help. We have a society of men sworn to rescue the girls. We can do what the law can't. Each of these men has lost a wife, a sister or a daughter. We're always ready to help."

The man applying bandages looked over at Chooli. "Hello, Chooli, my name is Sky. My girl was your age when she went for a walk and never returned. It heals my heart to see you safe."

Grace walked to the injured men. "Thank you. I'm at a loss for words to tell you how much you've done for me and my daughter. I'll pray every day that your loved ones will be returned to you."

Paul and Han were brought into the clearing on stretchers, followed by Arthur and David. Arthur called, "We've gotta get these two to help, fast. The hospital in Trinidad is fifteen minutes away."

Chooli ran to her father, "Dad! You came for me." She bent over her father, looked at his bleeding chest, and reached for his hand. "I love you, Dad."

Paul gasped for a breath. "I love you, too."

The stretchers were loaded in the back of a van with two other injured men. The rest of the men gathered in a tight circle to chant prayers.

Kiie pulled artificial pine branches off a hidden Jeep. He reached into the back and pulled out a small black bag. "Chooli, they put a chip in you, a locator device. Probably did it while you were drugged. Do you remember feeling sore anywhere?"

Chooli rubbed her left arm. "A cut, it bled for a while. Rose had a cut too."

He felt her arm. "Here it is, right under the skin. I can feel the bump. It's a small disk about the size of a pea."

"Take it out! I don't want it. Please take it out so they'll never find me again." She was sobbing.

"It'll hurt."

Chooli thrust out her arm. "Do it!"

Sally wrapped her arms around her granddaughter. "Her mother and I will hold her. She's strong, do it."

Grace looked at Kiie. "Take it out, I've got her too."

Chooli kept her arm out straight, her mouth set in a firm line. "I am not their prisoner anymore!"

He removed a sharp knife, bandages, and disinfectant from the first aid kit in the bag. He swabbed the knife and looked at Chooli. "Okay, on the count of three. One, two . . . " He thrust the tip of the knife into her skin, moved it under the object lodged there, and then nudged it forward and upward. Using tweezers from the kit, he pulled the disk out, dropped it on the ground and stomped on it. He applied ointment and wrapped a bandage around the wound. Chooli looked at him, her eyes open wide. But she had not made a sound.

They buried the device under a tree and got into the Jeep, leaving the woods and battleground behind.

After an hour's drive south, Sally saw familiar red rock formations. They were back on the Navajo Nation Reservation. Home.

Joyce Phillips

CHAPTER SEVENTEEN

"We're back on the Navajo Reservation. Where to next?" Kiie asked. He pulled over to the side of the road. Ahead, miles of seemingly uninhabitable land reached out to red-rock cliffs near Albuquerque. The engine purred. A fine dust blew in from the open side window. "I'm not familiar with your piece of the rez." His hands rested on the steering wheel.

The injured hawk next to Sally fluffed its feathers and screeched. She looked down into its eyes. "We can't go to my condo. A fire destroyed the back rooms. I suppose we could go to a hotel. We haven't been followed since we got rid of Chooli's tracking device. We'd be safe at the Albuquerque Hotel in Old Town. But will they allow our buddy here in as a pet?"

Grace leaned forward from the back seat. "I can give you directions, Kiie. We can go to my trailer. There's room for all of us. My friends will keep us safe." Grace looked at her sleeping daughter. "Chooli needs to feel secure again. Back in her own room. If we go into Albuquerque, it'll be noisy, with strange people all around. At home, she can sleep in her own bed. Give me your cell phone, I don't know where mine is. I'll call Ann."

Sally handed the phone over. "Here's my burner phone, Grace. I see only two bars. I don't know if that'll be enough to get through to Ann."

By some miracle, the call went through and Ann answered after two rings. Grace hit the speaker button so Chooli could hear. "Hello, are you alright? How's Chooli? Chau came to the prayer circle to spread the news that you rescued Chooli. Everyone was overjoyed to hear the good news. My husband came to get me and we were on our way home when Chau called to say there was a fire at your mother's condo. Apparently, someone threw a firebomb and the back in damaged. It'll be awhile before she can go back there. I checked your place. Your trailer and animals are fine. Are you on your way home?"

"Yes, we just crossed over into Navajo country. We'll be there in about an hour. Mom is staying with us and we have a new friend driving. We need room for him, too." The hawk screeched. "Oh, and we have another passenger. An injured hawk. Is it possible you can find someone to care for him?"

"I'll take care of it. When I came back, I cleaned your trailer. I'll call the Chapter house. I'm sure someone there knows an Elder who can care for the hawk. I can't wait to see you. I'll take care of everything here. Just come home."

Chooli leaned into her mother. "We're coming, Aunt Ann. Did you feed the chickens?"

"Yes, Chooli. I fed the chickens and your horse and brought your dog home with me. Everything is ready for you to come home."

"We're on our way. See you soon." Grace smiled when she ended the conversation. "Ann will notify my neighbors that we're coming home with Chooli."

Before getting back on the road, Sally called Chau. "We're on our way back. I'm planning to stay at Grace's trailer. What does the damage to my condo look like?"

"Not good. It'll be some time until you can move back in. You must all be worn out. If there's anything we can do for you, let me know. My friends send their love. We can help you and Mr. Li find a place to live until your condo is repaired."

"Han and Paul were injured at a camp in the Colorado woods. Mercenaries attacked us and there was a battle. Both men were shot. They're in a hospital in Trinidad, Colorado." Sally spoke in a quiet, reserved voice.

Chau growled, "Somehow, we gotta make them pay. They can't keep doing this. It's not over!"

Sally sighed. "It has to be for now. We need time to repair our minds and bodies. I'll be in touch. Tell your friends we're grateful for their help in bringing Chooli home." She shut down her phone, squared her shoulders and told Kiie, "Let's go."

Grace peered ahead. "We need to get on Route 491. It'll bring us south. We turn off before Gallup on Route 264 toward Window Rock. I live on a dirt road just after Window Rock. I'll tell you when." Traffic on reservation roads was sparse. They traveled mile after mile, only occasionally sighting a trailer or a cluster of trailers and *hogans*. When they arrived at Window Rock, Kiie stopped for gas and a bathroom break for his passengers.

When he turned onto the five-mile dirt road that led to Grace's trailer, Chooli reached in front to Sally. "We're almost there!" She sobbed. "I thought I'd never be back here, Grandma. Then I heard you in my dreams and knew you were coming to get me."

Sally held the girl's hand and brought it to her chest. "You were always in my heart. Look, nothing's changed here. The chickens have escaped from their pen again and are all over the front yard. Your mom's and dad's vehicles are parked in the back. It's the same trailer with the busted front porch railing your father hasn't fixed."

Kiie pulled to a stop in front of the trailer. "I'll go inside first. Just to make sure it's as empty as it looks from here. He walked up to the door, pulled it open, and stepped inside. His call of "Hello!" echoed throughout the kitchen, living room, and bedrooms. He returned to the Jeep and held the door open for Grace. "All's clear in there. There's a cardboard box on the counter in the kitchen. Looks like some food supplies and a bunch of mail for Chooli."

Grace said, "Come in, Kiie, stay with us. We have room. You can rest. I'll make us some tea and something to eat."

He shook his head. "I'll go back to the compound. They'll need help with the cleanup. I have your cell phone number, and I'll call when I have more news about your man. The last message from South Dakota was that the police had left the scene of the downed plane, and Hosteen was returning to his home on the rez. Our work isn't done. More than ever, we need to provide protection and safety for our girls."

"What about Han and Paul? Is there any way we can find out about them? I tried calling, but no bars," Sally asked.

Kiie nodded. "I'll go see the men in the hospital and tell them you're home. I'll get a message to you."

"Take me to them." Sally got out of the Jeep and faced Kiie. She placed a tentative hand on his arm. "I want to be with my husband."

"You should stay here and get your strength back. All of you look real beat up." Kiie shrugged. "I'll bring you, but it'll be a hard ride. Your choice."

After she got out of the Jeep, Chooli struggled to stand. She brushed her mother's hands aside and paced. Her face turned red and dark eyes blazed in agitation. "I want to see Dad. He's a hero. You said it was over. But it won't be until we're all together again." Her body quaked with the intensity of her words. Arms and hands moved in jerks to emphasize a fight with invisible people. Her feet beat a rhythm used when she ran. "He's, my father. He needs to be home, too. Go get him, Kiie, and bring him here."

Kiie grabbed her flailing hands. "Your dad is in the Mount San Rafael Hospital. People are caring for him. You need to rest." He moved to allow Grace to wrap her arms around her daughter and hold her steady.

Sally watched her family go through the front door of the trailer and settle on a sofa in the living room. Chooli huddled into her mother's arms. The hawk spread its good wing and hopped from the nest to settle down next to Chooli.

Her attention was centered on the two girls inside the open door, when Kiie nudged her and motioned Sally to join him in front of the trailer. He sat on a bench and patted the seat next to him for her to sit. He rubbed his face with a nervous hand before speaking. "I've seen this from our Vietnam veterans. They call it Post Traumatic Stress Syndrome. She'll need help. So will you and her mother. You were all traumatized by the past days and nights."

Sally raised her head to look at her family. "The Navajo will gather here. They'll nurture my daughter and granddaughter. They won't be alone. Their clan members will come. But Paul and Han are injured. In hospital beds in Trinidad. I need to be there with them." She stood and walked toward the open door. She stood inside the door and watched her daughter and granddaughter embrace.

"Mom, are you leaving with Kiie? So soon?" Grace untangled herself from her daughter's embrace and approached her mother. "I want to come with you, but I can't leave Chooli. Promise me you'll look after Paul for me."

Sally nodded. "Yes, we're leaving now. I need to be with Han, for him and for me. He's there because of his love for me."

She looked at Chooli. The girl had turned her attention to the injured hawk. She sat on the sofa, her arms wrapped around the bird, and whispered to it. "You're going to get better. We'll be friends."

"At least stay and eat. Look, a car is coming, they'll have food." Grace pointed at the dust cloud on their dirt road. A convoy of cars and trucks were headed for the trailer. "You have to at least wait until the road is clear again."

The caravan pulled into the driveway. Ann left her car in front of the trailer and ran to give Grace a hug. "I have food in the car. There's beef broth soup and egg sandwiches in the coolers." More neighbors arrived behind Ann. They parked their cars and trucks, got out, and nodded to Sally as they entered the trailer. The front room quickly filled with Navajo elders sitting peacefully. Sally remembered the Navajo vigil after Chooli's grandfather, Atza, died. They had sat in the same room to give support to the family. She had been new to Navajo traditions then. She couldn't speak their language, but their peaceful existence brought her comfort. They would do the same now and stay as long as anyone needed them.

Sally went looking for Chooli to say goodbye before leaving with Kiie. She found her in her own bedroom, sitting on her bed with the injured hawk.

Standing outside the bedroom door, scenes from the past days drifted past Sally's eyes. She remembered the last time she had stood with her granddaughter in this same room, practicing dance steps with her. They had hooted and laughed as their feet stomped a rhythm. Chooli had been a normal teenager only a few weeks ago. Today, she sat in her room calmly quieting a frightened bird after her return from days spent in caves as a prisoner, drugged, starved and abused by men. Sally whispered, "I don't know what lies ahead for you, Chooli. But I'll be with you."

She left Chooli's doorway and went to look for her daughter. "I'm going back with Kiie, Grace. I'll call you as soon as I know anything about Paul."

"Tell him I need him . . . tell him Chooli needs him." Grace stumbled. A man with turquoise beads hanging over a blue work shirt stood and caught her in his arms. "You must sit. Here, take my place." He helped her over to an empty place on the sofa.

"I promise I'll call as soon as I get to the hospital. I'll tell Paul." After long hugs goodbye, Sally followed Kiie to the Jeep.

A Navajo woman dressed in a traditional blouse and skirt smiled at Sally and pressed a basket of sandwiches and cookies into her hands.

Sally buckled her seat belt. Tears were threatening to fall. She turned to Kiie. "Let's go!"

The highway north continued across endless miles of Navajo Nation land. As their Jeep ate up each mile, Sally peered out the front window and allowed her tears to fall. She blew her nose on a blue handkerchief Kiie passed to her. "Here. You can let it all out now. Your job as a searcher is over. Chooli has a future because of you."

"Hosteen made it happen." She wrapped her fingers around the silver and turquoise bears hanging around her neck. "He's been with me from the beginning of the search. He knew how to help me find Chooli in a trance. He never gave up hope. Do you know him?"

"Yes. I've worked with Hosteen for years. We met when he searched for his wife's sister and I was looking for my wife. He continues to search for her. His wife needs her sister found so she can be whole again. Hosteen hopes that each new search will bring him to where the cartel has hidden his wife's twin."

Sally turned her head toward Kiie. "He told me about losing a twin sister during a trance. I saw a woman looking out a window at his trailer. When I asked him about her, he didn't answer me. Is his wife the twin sister?"

"She lives with him, but is not a wife anymore. He cares for her every need. She cannot speak. His sister comes to care for her when he is gone. It's been many years." Kiie took his eyes off the road for a moment to stare at Sally. "You must never speak of her. Look, Shiprock's ahead."

Tiny peaks in the distance emerged to become an image of a sailing ship. "Chooli told me about Shiprock being the Sacred Peak of the Navajo people. She explained her ancestral people believed a bird carried them on its back from a distant land. The Navajo call it the rock with wings. I wish I could fly to my husband."

The Jeep suddenly swerved to the right onto the gravel side strip for a moment before Kiie pulled the vehicle straight again.

"Are you OK driving? It's been two days now . . . maybe we should stop." Sally saw Kiie's eyes were red rimmed.

"We're picking up a driver in Shiprock. Not far. I can't sleep, but I need fresh eyes for the road. Don't worry, we'll get to the hospital safe." His eyes left the road for an instant and looked at the food basket between them. "You know, I could use another water and one of those cookies. Nothing better than Navajo cookies." He cracked a faint smile on dry lips.

Sally placed another bottle of water in his beverage holder and a cookie. "I think these cookies may have been laced with native herbs to calm our minds." She took a swallow from her bottle. "I owe you and your friends a lifetime of thanks for what you've done for my family. How long have you been doing this?"

He crunched on the cookie. "You figured it out? Arthur had the family campground in the woods for years. We met in a bar six months after they found his wife's body. My wife had been missing for three years back then." He stopped talking and shook his head. He took a deep breath and said, "We made a promise to our wives we'd do what we could for their sisters. Others have joined since then. Each has his own reason for fighting. We've been getting the girls back when we can for several years. Hosteen sometimes can locate them when there's a family connection. Like yours. But it gets worse all the time. Nobody pays attention to the missing girls. They don't see the dead bodies . . . so many of them. We only find a few." He took a deep breath. "Every one of the missing counts. We all share the same blood. Don't people see that?" He blinked, then took another slug from his water bottle.

When he raised the last question, his voice took on a tremor. She reached over to touch his hand on the steering wheel. "Books barely covered Native history when I was in school. Even today, little information makes the news about Native people. People don't know about the missing girls in New Mexico or South Dakota. My granddaughter is free because of you and your friends. There must be something I can do." Sally squirmed as she tried to comprehend why an atrocity in America continued to be ignored.

Kiie's fist hit the steering wheel. "Tell them! Tell them all! Let America know, but be careful. It's not over for you. You saw a lot more of the ugly world these past days than anyone should. You may not feel it now, but you'll need counseling for post-traumatic stress. And you made yourself a target on the low life's radar when you were at the rescue scene. Your Chinese husband and your blonde hair are easy to spot. If I were you, I'd disappear along with your Navajo family."

Another fifteen minutes and Kiie pulled into a rest stop on the south side of Shiprock. As the Jeep approached, a blue Ford pickup flashed its headlights. A man jumped down from the passenger side, ran around in front of the truck, and opened Kiie's door.

"Ready for some shut-eye, old man?" The young Navajo asked. "You've been awake way too long. I'll take over."

"Sally, this mouthy lad is my nephew, Broadwing. He'll bring us to the hospital in Trinidad where your men are. Two of our guys got shot and are there too. Got any good words for us, Nephew?"

"Our friends wounds were treated, and they've been released. But the others, the Navajo and Chinese man, are still critical. They wait for you." The boy's dark eyes held Sally's. "Your man calls out for you. He will heal. The other waits. His lungs have blood. My people say prayers there."

Sally moved to the back seat as Kiie changed over to the front passenger side. Broadwing got behind the wheel and looked at the food basket. He grabbed a cookie and took a bite.

"Good! Navajo made. They'll sustain us for the rest of the journey." He waved at the pickup and drove the Jeep back onto the road.

Sally asked, "How long until we get to the hospital? Have you seen the men?"

"We're still a long way from Colorado. An hour or more. You rest back there. I've my cell phone on, so we'll get a message if there're any changes. My friends are in the waiting area. Your men are in ICU, no visitors." He turned toward Kiie. "Sleep, Uncle. I'll bring us the rest of the way."

Sally found a pillow on the back seat and put it behind her head. She leaned back and closed her eyes.

CHAPTER EIGHTEEN

A sudden jolt caused Sally's head to fall off the pillow. She opened her eyes to the entrance of a brightly lit hospital building. Broadwing opened the doors for her and Kiie. "I'll park this thing and join you inside."

The one-story white adobe building sat on the edge of a parking lot filled with cars, pickup trucks, and ambulances. A sign above the entrance read Trinidad Memorial Hospital. A half-moon hung over a log *hogan* to the east of the hospital. Steady drum beats reverberated from inside. Sally stopped in front of the *hogan*. "Kiie, the drum beats are steady. It sounds like a heartbeat. Does it mean our men are alive?" She put her hand on her heart to feel the rhythm of her own heartbeat.

Kiie nodded. "The drum talks for our men inside. Come, we will find out how they are." He walked toward the glass doors at the entrance. Inside a brightly lit lobby, men stood and sat on chairs. They gathered at the door as Sally approached. As it slid open, Sally froze. "I can't go in Kiie. I can't."

"We gotta go inside." Kiie reached for her arm.

"Wait, I'll move the guys inside. They're crowding the door." Broadwing jogged in front of Sally and swept his arms around, backing the men away from the door. He turned and waved for them to come.

"What if . . . ? I'm afraid . . . Can't move. My legs don't work." She swayed and reached for Kiie.

"You can't quit now. He's inside. Come on. I'll go with you." Kiie wrapped an arm around her waist and led her through the open door to the reception desk. A gray-haired woman rushed from behind her desk. The badge on her chest read, "Emily Wood, Volunteer." She pushed a chair toward Sally. "Here, sit down. I'll call for a doctor."

"No, not me. My husband's here, Han Li, he was shot." She burst out crying and collapsed with a thud into the offered chair. "My son-in-law, Paul Begay, is here too." She tried to stand, but her shaky legs gave in and she fell back into the chair. "Please, I need to see them."

The volunteer returned to her desk and typed on her computer. "I'll have someone bring you."

A man wearing white pants and shirt jogged down the hallway, pushing a wheelchair. "Hello, I'm Jefferson, I'll bring you to your husband. His doctor is here and will meet us in your husband's room. Emily said you should use this."

The wheelchair stopped in front of Sally. She stood. Then sat again. "Kiie, I'm afraid. I don't know if I can do this. Hospitals scare me."

"Come on, I'll go with you." Kiie took a red plaid handkerchief from his back pocket and swabbed at her face.

"Dry your tears. You've been tough, just a little longer." He took her arm and eased her into the wheelchair.

Jefferson brought them up one corridor, made a left turn down another, and stopped in front of a room at the end of the hall. "Are you ready? Both men are here."

Inside, green walls surrounded two beds containing her husband and Paul. White blankets covered their still bodies. Instrument panels over their heads flashed colors, monitoring their heart rates with ceaseless mountain peaks and valleys. Numbers off to the side blinked, IV bags hung from standing poles. Tubes ran into arms. Once healthy faces were ashen. Paul had more tubes that led under the blanket. His eyes were open. His chest rose and fell with agonizing growls.

Sally looked at Han. His eyes were closed. She rose from the wheelchair and went first to Paul, put her hand on his. His eyes moved toward her. She squeezed his hand. "They're home. Safe. Neighbors are with them."

He mouthed words, "Tell them . . ." Then stopped to gasp for breath. After a moment, he said, "It's not over. Go!" Then more Navajo words.

Kiie stepped forward. "I'll tell them. They're okay. You sleep now." He turned to Sally and whispered, "I'll tell you later. Go to your man."

At Han's bedside, she leaned over to kiss his forehead. A kiss they shared when not alone and speaking of love.

When they met, the English and Mandarin words and customs were foreign to each of them. Americans kissed in public. In China, Han found it difficult to show affection in front of people, so they had communicated affection with a kiss on the forehead. Their private expression of love.

"Sally." He opened his eyes and managed a weak smile. "You got here. I'm okay. Doctor said I did good for an old man."

A voice from behind her interjected. "Yes, he came out of surgery in good shape. A bullet went into his left shoulder, tore some of the pectoral muscle, and he lost a lot of blood."

When Sally turned, she saw a man that appeared young enough to still be in school.

"I'm American now, have American blood." Han looked at the Doctor. "When can I go?"

The freckle faced, red-haired man held out his hand to Sally. "Hello, I'm Doctor McAdams. I removed the bullets from your husband and son-in-law." He stepped forward to peer into Han's face.

"Mr. Li, I took the bullet out less than six hours ago. You have quite a bit of American blood, and I need to keep you here for a while longer. The wound is deep, your arm needs time to heal. You also have three broken ribs and a compound wrist fracture." He tapped the chart in his hand. "You should make a full recovery. Give it time. I've sent out a search for an acupuncturist for you. Never done that before."

Sally looked at the doctor. "I've seen it work for pain in China."

The doctor smiled. "Acupuncture wasn't covered in our medical rotations. I got to admit I wasn't sure, but after some investigation, it seems there's significant evidence- based research on acupuncture's effectiveness. I'm all for a marriage of Eastern and Western medicine." His face turned red. "Your marriage looks good."

A gasp from the other bed turned the doctor's head toward Paul. He walked over and peered at the numbers showing on the screens. "He took a bullet to the chest and has a pulmonary embolism. We're draining fluid from his lungs."

Sally turned to Han. "I'll be back. Just need to talk to Paul. I've messages for him from Grace and Chooli."

She sat on Paul's bed and held his hand. Fluid in his lungs meant his heart could stop at any moment. Leaning over, she looked into his eyes and said, "If you hadn't brought warriors to the camp, the fight would've had a different ending. You saved your wife and daughter's lives. Grace sends love. She's home, exhausted and caring for Chooli. Your daughter is a brave warrior, like her father. She said you will ride your horses together when you return. Your neighbors are with them."

He raised himself off the pillow. "Tell them I love them." He groaned and began to sing. The blinking lights on the machines attached to him went out. The doctor ran to his side and pulled back the sheet covering his chest, but Kiie stopped him. "No, no resuscitation." He reached for Paul's hand and sang the last notes of his friend's death song.

Sally watched his heart line run flat across the screen.

The doctor broke the ensuing silence. "Time of death, 7:59 p.m."

Sally gave Paul's hand a last squeeze, then placed it on his chest. Bending over, she whispered in his ear, "You are a brave man. Go now to a better place."

Kiie held the doctor's eyes. "He knew he would not survive; he asked me to help him with his last sing. Sorry I stopped you from reviving him, Doc. He's a brother, it was his time." He nodded at the doctor. "We need to move him from here. His *Chindi* will come. The Navajo believe that an evil ghost appears after someone dies and causes harm to the living. Paul would not want to cause something bad happening to the other man."

Sally turned toward Dr. McAdams. "I want to bring him home. He'll be buried there, and his family needs to say goodbye." She stumbled as she rose. "I don't feel good." Then she pitched forward into the doctor's arms.

"What happened? Sally! Is she alright?" Han struggled to get up from his bed. Alarms rang in his machines. A nurse ran into the room. Another behind her. An announcement sounded. "Code Red."

The room filled with anxious people. Dr. McAdams said, "She fainted. Bring a wheelchair." His voice of authority brought the pandemonium under control. With a dose of hospital smelling salts, Sally opened her eyes. A blood pressure test followed. "You're dehydrated and stressed. Drink water and stay here a while." The doctor wheeled her next to Han, picked up his chart from the bottom of the bed and wrote on it. "I'm making a note that Mr. Li has a new attending care giver." He put the chart away and informed the pair. "Your wife is the best medicine I can order for you."

The alarms silenced when Sally returned to Han's bedside and reached for his hand. "I plan to stay here until we leave together. The rest of the world can take care of themselves."

A nurse pulled the curtain across Paul's bed. Another nurse entered the room and voices lowered to quiet murmurs behind the curtain.

"What's next?" Han asked. "The evil people are defeated."

Kiie walked over. "They aren't defeated. There are more. The slave trade is too lucrative. Girls are constantly moved. Mexican cartels pay good money, but also bordellos up north. Missing Indian girls get little publicity, not like a missing blond, blue-eyed girl does. Indigenous lives are not valued. My people will bring Paul back to his family. Your wife needs to stay with you, and you need to make plans to get away from here. Far away." He took Han's hand. "I'm going to find a Tai Chi teacher. It was my honor to work with you." He turned and left the room.

Han's eyes closed, and his breath slowed. The mountains and valleys on his heart monitor were steady. He slept.

Nurses wrapped Paul in a body bag and brought him from the hospital room on a gurney pushed by an orderly wearing a name tag: Nighthawk Begay. His stretcher moved down the hall as nurses, doctors, and visitors stood shoulder to shoulder along the passage to honor a Navajo hero.

Sally watched from her wheelchair at the open doorway. She held her cell phone in her hand to record the stirring event. She whispered a commentary for Grace as the gurney disappeared down the hall. "Paul is leaving the hospital with dignity. He'll be back with you in a day. Kiie arranged for his nephew, Broadwing, to bring him to you. The show of respect here is amazing. I'm so proud of my son-in-law."

Back in the room, she put her hands to her face and sobbed. An arm wrapped around her shoulders and brought her face next to a broad chest. Kiie said, "You can cry now. He'll be home soon."

"He saved us, Kiie. He saved his daughter and wife. Will the Navajo bury him with the dignity he deserves? Will they know what he did?"

"They know. He'll be sent away with Navajo honor. My nephew will make sure. Come back in the room. I need to go down to talk with the assembled Navajo out front." Kiie led her back to Han.

The phone vibrated with an incoming call. The screen showed Chau's face in front of a background of the University of New Mexico computer experts. A chorus of "Hello's" sounded when she pushed the on button.

"Are the men good? When are you coming back?" Chau's words were rushed, his voice strained.

"Han is okay, but I need to stay here with him. His injuries were severe, but the doctor says he will make a full recovery. It may be a while before we're back. What's happening there?"

Melinda said, "Good! Stay where you are. We found threats on the dark web. The fire at your condo was a warning. They want Chooli back. And they want you."

Sally's hand shook in an uncontrolled spasm. She gripped the phone with her left hand and bent forward to hold on to her stomach. A sick feeling was threatening to explode. "Are you safe? Where are you?"

"We're safe! In Albuquerque. We scrubbed the laptops we used in your condo clean. They won't come after us, too much of a chance of publicity. Stories of missing native women and girls are sprouting all over the internet. Not just the dark web anymore, news of Chooli's rescue has spread, bringing hope to silent families."

Sally asked, "Have you been in touch with Grace? I have sad news for her. Paul didn't survive."

Melinda's face became distressed. "I'm sorry. He was a good man. No, we haven't heard from the reservation."

"Thank you for your news. Please, take care of yourselves. Our journey together has been empowering, I see a future full of promise with young people like you as leaders. I'll stay in touch. Chau, I trust we will have a long relationship ahead." A chorus of goodbyes followed. Sally smiled as she hung up.

Cell phone service to the reservation was always iffy, Sally hoped this time she would get through. Grace answered immediately. "Mom, are you with Paul? Is he okay?" Her face on the phone screen looked haggard.

Sally took a deep breath. She had to relay bad news that she wished could be done in person. "Grace, I'm at the Trinidad Memorial Hospital in Colorado. I have sad news for you. Paul was badly injured. He was shot in his chest at close range, and blood congealed in his lungs. His heart stopped, and he passed away minutes ago."

Grace's face disappeared from the phone. A loud keening erupted. Her pain reverberated across the miles that separated them. When she returned, she said, "Did you see him? Did he hurt?"

The phone was her connection to her daughter when she wanted to be there herself. Sally answered, "The doctor said he didn't have pain or difficulty breathing. He told me he loved you and Chooli. He sang his last song with Kiie. I'm so sorry."

"What now?"

"The Navajo here will bring Paul back to you. I plan to stay here with Han. He will get better. He was badly hurt; I need to be with him."

Sally listened to murmurs from Grace's phone. "How is Chooli?"

Chooli's face appeared. "Dad died?"

"Yes, I'm sorry Chooli. Your father was a hero. He died in the hospital ten minutes ago. He was shot in his chest. He lost a lot of blood. I held his hand. Chooli, he wanted you to remember he loved you and was proud of you. We will talk when I see you but I'm going to stay in the hospital with my husband until we can leave together. How are you?"

"I have nightmares. Mom slept with me last night. When are you coming back?"

"Han was badly hurt. I want to stay here with him. We will come to see you together."

When the phone conversation ended, Sally went to Han, eased his lifelines to the side, and crawled onto his bed. She slept.

CHAPTER NINETEEN

One year later

A satisfying slam of the screen door announced Chooli's return. "Grandma, I'm home. We biked all the way to Dennis and back. You said that was ten miles. Can I have a cookie?"

"Yes, you may. And I've made a pitcher of sun tea." Sally walked out to the kitchen of her Cape Cod cottage and gave her granddaughter a hug. She never tired of feeling the closeness of her precious child.

She had missed Chooli's first thirteen years and almost lost her forever a year ago when kidnappers abducted her at the Cottonwood Mall in Albuquerque. After the ordeal was over, to escape the human predators after Chooli, Sally brought her family from New Mexico to settle on Cape Cod.

Each day that Sally stayed in the hospital with her husband injured in the fight with kidnappers had seemed like an eternity. Han healed from his shoulder wound. His cracked ribs took longer, and each breath came with a gasp. Doctors explained that his years in China with polluted air had left scars on his lungs and that, combined with his recent injury, resulted in COPD. They advised him to leave the high-altitude area. Cape Cod's highest altitude point is 306 feet above sea level. A ready solution for his breathing was a move to Sally's home on the cape.

"How about helping me with the garden?" Sally asked. "I have guests' due tomorrow and want fresh flowers for their room."

That caught the teenager's attention. "Who's coming? Where're they from?"

"A mother and daughter from Arizona. They'll be here for two weeks. Gertie said they need to escape the confines of the reservation." Sally turned toward Chooli. "It's strange that reservations of hundreds of miles can hold secrets so tight that a feeling of freedom is destroyed. Here, our space is measured in feet, yet the Atlantic Ocean cures a broken mind with her salt air and tidal pull."

"How old is the girl?" Chooli poured herself a glass of ice tea and sat at the kitchen table. "I hope Gertie and Walter come again soon. Walter is the bomb. He knows all the cool music."

"Maybe later this fall. I miss them too. They stay busy visiting the Navajo Reservation and the Rosebud in South Dakota. The girl's name is Francien, she's 14. That's all I know about them." Sally sat at the table across from Chooli. Her hand reached for her granddaughter's. Her concern for her own precious family reliving agonizing memories was always forefront in her mind when she accepted new guests from out west to her bed-and-breakfast.

"Maybe she'll have dance steps she can show me. Mom says I can use the different dances in a documentary on our cultural similarities." Chooli squeezed her grandmother's hand. "I'm good. Don't worry, showing the dances is excellent exercise. I'll get your flowers and then go home to check my email messages."

Home had once been Sally's garage. After the four arrived on Cape Cod, Sally hired a local carpenter to enlarge her garage and make a two-bedroom cottage for Grace and Chooli. Grace found work with the Barnstable County Housing Assistance. She applied for a transfer of her law degree and was waiting for the next bar exam so she could practice in Massachusetts. Soon after they arrived on the Cape, Grace dived into women's rights and often went to Boston to work incognito on the worldwide epidemic of human trafficking.

The odd foursome of a Chinese man with a blonde wife and a Navajo mother and daughter had drawn some attention when they moved in, but soon news of Great White sharks and thousands of seals eating fish and pooping in the ocean had garnered the media attention. They became old news and neighbors granted them privacy.

Sally's cottage was three bedrooms and two baths when she returned to the Cape with Han. The talented carpenter also added a wing in the back with an additional bedroom and bath so she could rent out two rooms. Advertised as a B&B, her guests primarily were from the west, girls who needed to escape.

~~~~~

"How was your day?" Han asked, as he opened the picnic basket on their beach blanket.

Sally sipped her wine and watched the white-capped waves roll onto shore. "Every day I spend with you and my family is wonderful. Look, we have a red sunset tonight."

"Red skies in the evening, sailors delight, red skies in the morning sailors take warning," Han recited. He had found a job teaching Chinese history at Cape Cod Community College shortly after they arrived and taught Mandarin at the high school Adult Education Classes.

They spent many evenings together at the beach watching the wonder of the ocean as the tides moved the water and the seagulls called to friends.

Other Books by Joyce Phillips

About the Author

A desire to write a story about my life for my grandchildren became a Memoir, The Life That Made Me, ME, in 2016. I wrote some family history, my philosophy on life, about people who influenced who I am today, and stories of my travels.

At the end of the book, I wrote about my three-week backpacking trip to China with three other ladies. One story about China became a book of a retired schoolteacher finding romance while traveling in China.

Sally is the star character in China Strong and Navajo Strong, my second novel. While writing Navajo Strong, I came across a newspaper story about the missing and murdered indigenous girls and women in the west. I knew that would be my next book. COVID and the sudden loss of my son delayed my third novel.

I spent nights dreaming of Scott, feeling the pain of my loss. The next morning, I sat in front of my computer writing and rewriting the story of a mother's, and grandmother's loss of a child. Their heartache, and Chooli's fear, became real.

Joyce Phillips

Stolen Sisters is the third book in Sally's trilogy and a stand-alone mystery/thriller.

ACKNOWLEDGMENTS

I am a volunteer at the West Dennis Library on Cape Cod. Once a week, I browse the contemporary novels and decide which ones I will bring home. So many writing styles and ideas. Each author encourages me to tell my story.

My fur baby at home is a Siamese cat who tells me when it's time for me to stop writing and take care of her. We have an understanding that a treat will appear when I finish a day's work. Her treat is a few Temptations, and mine is ice cream.

I am grateful for members of two writer's groups who have encouraged me to continue writing. Rising Tide Writers meet weekly and listened as I read each new chapter. We Write Stuff encouraged me to continue with the nerve-wracking process of building my story from an idea to a book.

A special thanks to my editor, Carol March in Albuquerque, for helping me to realize a polished manuscript.

CPSIA information can be obtained
at www.ICGtesting.com
Printed in the USA
JSHW010317110423
40165JS00002B/12